Acclaim for Christopher Meeks's
The Middle-Aged Man and the Sea
and Other Stories:

"A collection that is so stunning...that I could not help but move on to the next story."
— *Entertainment Weekly*

"Poignant and wise, sympathetic to the everyday struggles these characters face."
— *Los Angeles Times*

"These are original, articulate, engaging stories which examine life in America from the unique perspectives of ordinary people searching for their share of the promises held out as part of the American dream. ... *The Middle-Aged Man & The Sea* is highly recommended, highly entertaining, and highly rewarding reading."
— *The Midwest Book Review*

"Christopher Meeks bounces onto the literary scene as a vibrant new voice filled with talent and imagination. *The Middle-Aged Man and the Sea* is one of the finer collections of short stories that will rapidly rise to the top to of the heap of a battery of fine writers of this difficult medium."
— **Grady Harp, Top Ten Reviewer, Amazon.com**

"Mr. Meeks has a wonderfully fun writing style—witty, cynical, and often poignant. His stories are about the stuff of life: love and heartbreak, sickness and death, desires and struggles, spirituality and the search for meaning."
— **Janet Rubin,** *Novel Reviews*

"In this collection of short stories, Christopher Meeks examines the small heartbreaks and quiet despair that are so much a part of all of our lives. He does it in language that is resonant, poetic, and precise. Franz Kafka said that a book should be an ice-axe to break the frozen sea within us. This collection is just such a weapon. If you like Raymond Carver, you'll love Meeks. He may be as good—or better. He deserves major recognition."
— **author David Scott Milton** (*Paradise Road*)

"If the publishing and reading world is fair and just, Christopher Meeks is destined to be widely read and deservedly honored."
   — **Carolyn Howard-Johnson, Myshelf.com**

"Many of these tales have appeared in American literary journals, but reading them together, you get the full impact of Meeks's talent, as he takes you in a head-long assault through ordinary day-to-day life, the mundane under the microscope and given the once-over through Meeks's careful eye."
   — **Susan Tomaselli, *Dogmatika***

"While Ellis and the other characters in Meeks's stories are in one way or another, and to varying degrees, 'Californicated' ...they and the stories that contain them are firmly rooted in this universe where the only magic available to save any of them is the only kind available to save any of us: self-awareness and self-discipline."
   —**David Reilly, *Lance Mannion***

Books by Christopher Meeks

The Middle-Aged Man and the Sea and Other Stories

Who Lives? (A Drama)

Months and Seasons and Other Stories

ISBN 978-0-6151-8870-6
Library of Congress Control Number: 2008922108
Copyright © 2008 by Christopher Meeks
First Edition

Library of Congress Cataloging-in-Publication Data

Meeks, Christopher.
Months and seasons / by Christopher Meeks – 1st ed.
    p. cm.
    1. United States – Social life and customs – 21st century—
Fiction.
    PS3613.E374 M53 2008
    813.6

Editor, Nomi Isak Kleinmuntz

Book & Cover Design, Daniel Will-Harris,
                www.will-harris.com

Cover photo by Stefan Hermans, www.perrush.be

Published by White Whisker Books, Los Angeles, 2008

To Ann Pibel

and to the memory

of her mother,

Marie Franco.

Months
And
Seasons

And Other Stories

by Christopher Meeks

White Whisker Books
Los Angeles

Contents

Months And Seasons 7

Contents 8

Dracula Slinks Into The Night 9

The Farms at 93rd and Broadway 23

Catalina 36

The Sun Is a Billiard Ball 39

A Shoe Falls 71

The Holes In My Door 80

The Old Topanga Incident 92

A Whisker 101

Months And Seasons 109

The Wind Just Right 122

Breaking Water 129

Bonus Track: "The Hand" 154

"The Hand" 155

Acknowledgements: 170

"Dracula Slinks Into the Night" first appeared as an Amazon Short and was reprinted in *Rosebud*.

"The Sun is a Billiard Ball" first appeared as an Amazon Short.

"The Holes in My Door" first appeared as an Amazon Short.

Dracula Slinks Into The Night

A bright orange envelope came addressed to "The Ghouls of the House." I ripped it open to find a card with Diane Arbus's famous black-and-white photo of twin seven-year-old girls in white tights, prim dresses, and wide headbands standing shoulder-to-shoulder with a thought bubble saying, "Hey, Tony! Where're you goin'?" Next to them as part of a collage, actor Tony Perkins dangled keys in front of Hitchcock's *Psycho* house and said, "To Randolph and Eloise's Halloween costume party." Inside, the invitation gave the date, address, and time. It was in one month.

I liked parties, but, come on: costume? I was forty-two. Besides, that weekend I would have a big contract to write as well as unfair labor practices to consider. My firm specialized in labor law. Workers were getting screwed in this country with more and more labor going to Mexico, India, and other less-developed countries, and unions were getting bashed. The grocery store clerks, specifically, were renegotiating their contract, and healthcare was a big issue once again. Health was everything.

Also inside the party invitation were the words, "Come dance until you drop...dead!" I wasn't in the mood. Of course, my wife Kathleen liked this kind of stuff despite her job, and Eloise was her best friend from work. Kathleen was the administrative assistant to a director of Forest Lawn, a cemetery in Los Angeles. Actually, it was called a memorial park, and a quartet of Forest Lawns dotted Los Angeles like birthmarks. Kathleen's job included taking on special assignments of a delicate nature brought to the director. She recently had to deal with a set of parents whose son had died from a fall during a wild weekend in Las Vegas, and the parents wanted to harvest sperm from their dead son—for a grandchild. Kathleen had to arrange the rush delivery of the body from Las Vegas to Los Angeles for the sperm harvester. Sperm, Kathleen learned, lived for three or more days after a man's death, and the parents had already found a surrogate mother—someone willing to open herself to a dead guy. This is why I try not to ask my wife each day how work was. The specifics can give me nightmares.

I heard the garage door open below. Moments later, Kathleen appeared at the top of the stairs, black boots and purple skirt, and she held her thin briefcase and her large black purse as if carrying a load of coal. She looked tired. However, when she saw me, she gave a smile. Her face became a musical rest note. This reminded me of one of the many reasons I loved living with her: she could be cheerful, even under pressure. When she saw the invitation, she said, "How fun! You want to go, don't you?" Granted, I was late at the marriage game, having waited until I hit forty, and Kathleen was ten years my junior, closer to youth, but if I knew one thing, it was to proceed with caution in these matters.

"That's a tricky weekend," I said. "I'd like to go, but the labor contract will be heating up, and I might even have to meet with the negotiating committee."

"Nothing says you have to drink," she said. Her hopeful-ness made it seem as if the costume party was crucial to our marriage. I saw a twinkle in her eye, and I was as smitten with her now as I had been on our blind date.

"It's not that," I said. "You know I like to have fun with you."

"I'm starting to wonder. When was the last time you truly let go?"

"There was Catalina." As I said it, I remembered how even then I'd spent a lot of time on the laptop.

"Hugh," was all she replied.

"Once I make partner—"

"Not that again!"

"It's important."

"So are babies," she said, running her finger around my ear, taking another tack.

There, I fell into it again. Despite my law degree, my skills were no match for Kathleen's. Soon she might be humming a song and dancing around me. Maybe she'd even sing spontane-ously again about her biological time clock. Hey, I wanted kids, but first things first. Quickly I said, "Okay, okay. The party sounds fun."

"Could you pretend that I'm a jury and you're trying to per-suade me?"

"I'm sorry," I said. "I'd *love* to go with you to the costume party."

She looked at me suspiciously. "You'd *love* to go? And you'll wear a costume?"

"I'll see what they have at the 99 Cents Store."

She laughed. "Figures."

A costume party should cost no more than 99 cents, but I decided not to say that out loud.

The next weekend on a Saturday, we drove to our respec-tive stores in separate cars. I found that while the 99 Cents Store had costumes, they were basically iconographic. A pirate hat made you a pirate. A tiara made you a princess. And, hey, a black cape made you Dracula. I could wear black jeans, a black shirt and shoes, and maybe a little gel in my hair to slick it back. Voila—a fabulous Dracula!

Kathleen returned home an hour after I did with two bags and a huge smile on her face. "Want to see?" she said.

She pulled out what had been an elegant white wedding gown, but it was full of holes and black streaks as if she had exhumed it at Forest Lawn. The bag also had a bouquet of dead flowers and a grungy garland for her head. Maybe she'd spent less than I had, after all.

She then held the dress in front of her. It was strapless, and bones had been painted on the side to show a fleshless rib cage. This costume wasn't from a dump. "So what are you going to be?" I asked.

"The Corpse Bride."

I shrugged. I'd never heard of such a thing.

"It's a movie." From her other bag, she pulled out a packet that said, *Official Corpse Bride Makeup Kit.* "It's approved by Tim Burton," she explained. "And it comes with a Burton-approved overskirt train, a wig of yarn twist strands, and everything!"

"They always jack up the price when there's a licensing agreement. Dracula, on the other hand, is in the public domain."

She licked her lips sensuously. "You shall be in my domain," she commanded with glee and moved her eyebrows up and down like Groucho Marx.

Yikes. This woman was amazing. I froze, however, when she added, "Just have fun. You've got to learn to let it go."

"Sure," I said, stuck on the thought that my wife saw me as tight. Had I become a workaholic? I could have fun. Not at that moment, however. I had a videoconference to attend shortly.

On the night of the party, I grabbed my new digital camera from the car. It offered a high ASA rating, which meant I could shoot in low light, and there surely would be tricky lighting and unusual people. As we approached the house in Pasadena, we could hear booming music, and as we turned the corner, I stopped, dumbfounded at the sight. Standing in front of the two-story Craftsman home, taller than the structure, was a human skeleton wearing a tall striped hat like the Cat in the Hat. Three fresh graves with headstones rested on the lawn, and one had the inscription of "You." A giant 3-D skull twirled at the peak of the house, a projection of a hologram. Music blasted everywhere. Fun, I thought.

"Where's the hologram's projector?" I asked. "How did Randolph do that?"

"I don't know," Kathleen said, a number of steps away from me. Her long dark-haired wig blended into the darkness, and her pale white makeup made her look ghostly. "He's a genius. Let's go."

Randolph, Eloise's husband, worked at JPL and had been an engineer on the Mars Rover missions. When one of the landers had crashed due to a simple miscalculation, he had told us over drinks, "Oops."

"How do you think he built such a large skeleton?" I wondered. "Are there kits for this? How does it stand?" I tried to look for bracing.

"I thought you didn't like Halloween."

"This is an engineering marvel."

"Let's get inside already."

I paused and photographed the scene with wide shots, close-ups, and different angles. When I was finished, I saw Kathleen impatiently waiting with that look on her face.

We entered the house going up a few steps. The front porch had been walled in with bricks since the last time we visited. It was odd there were no windows in it. We walked into the open front door. The living room, devoid of all furniture, was entirely a dance floor, undulating with costumed figures that included winged bats, a white-faced Geisha, a revolutionary soldier, an Egyptian princess with jet-black hair, and a man whose head was inside an aquarium. The aquarium had suspended fish and kelp and an eerie blue light from the top. Against one wall of the living room, a high-definition video projector cast moving abstract imagery like something from the sixties.

The awe I had felt outside vanished. These were adults with too much time on their hands. And didn't they know that the projector, sound system, and speakers were all Japanese? Their dancing shoes were probably from Mexico or China. America's jobs were going elsewhere and Americans were just dressing up and playing like kids. Gas prices were high. General Motors was going broke and laying off thousands—and these people were dancing.

"Let's find the hosts," said Kathleen, looking excited.

In the kitchen, we found our friends, a tall slender man and a much shorter woman. Normally she was blond. "Howdy, partner!" said Eloise, who was dressed as a cowgirl in a white shirt, red hat, chaps, and crimson hair with a matching long fake ponytail. She and Kathleen hugged as if they hadn't seen each other in weeks, even though it had been just hours. Eloise looked me up and down and chose not to comment and simply hugged me, too. "Nice that you two could make it."

"Wouldn't have missed it for anything," I said and glanced at Kathleen, who only smiled and shook her head.

"And I can't wait to get her on the dance floor." At that Eloise guffawed. Clearly, they'd spoken. Women seem to talk to each other about their men the way guys speak in well-considered analysis about football. Of course, I've never talked about football. I never understood a game with a ball that looked like a loaf of bread.

"Hey, Hugh," said Randolph who shook my hand, as friendly as always, then hugged Kathleen. He sported old-fashioned mutton chop sideburns and a mustache that connected. He must have spent months growing it. His diamond-checked sweater vest over a white shirt clashed with his plaid pants, and he wore a short-billed beret.

"What are you supposed to be?" I asked.

"Hoot, mon, what you reckon we go to the 19th hole?"

Only then did I notice he had a short golf club in his hand. "A Scottish golfer?"

"At the original golf course in St. Andrews, mon." He did his best to sound like Sean Connery, but he came across more like Jamaican Bob Marley. Randolph held up a golf ball. "The dimple pattern maximizes lift while minimizing drag." Leave it to an engineer to love that fact.

"Have fun!" said Eloise, taking Randolph by the hand and moving back into their party.

"Drinks and food are out back," said Randolph before disappearing. "And pies and desserts are in the dining room as you may have already seen."

"Food," I said.

"Dance," said Kathleen.

"I want to eat first."

"We ate before we came here. You said you'd dance."

"How about a drink? Let's have a drink."

"You always do this."

"What?"

"Do things your way."

"What're you talking about? We're at a party."

"Never mind," she said. "I'll wait. I always do."

She waited in the kitchen as I grabbed two Heinekens out back. Kathleen took the beer when I returned. She said nothing and just drank the beer. Women are as mysterious as comets.

After a slice of blueberry pie, my favorite, and another beer, I was feeling good enough to attack the dance floor and make a fool of myself.

As we danced on the dance floor to an old 10,000 Maniacs song, "These Are Days," Kathleen looked sexy in her low-cut gown. She moved and body-flirted with me, her fingers running down my arm. It was as if we were dating again. I bounced with my college-best motions. With the volume high, the female singer shouted:

> *These are days that you'll remember*
> *When May is rushing over you*
> *With desire to be part of the miracles.*

We sashayed to the side where the speakers weren't connected to our heads. "I vant to drink your blood," Kathleen said in her best Transylvanian accent.

"That's my line," I said. "I'm Dracula."

Keeping the accent, she said, "Maybe you vant to rock my bones."

"I vant to all the time," I replied, mimicking her. "But ve can't here."

"Vy not? Ze bathroom?"

"Did you bring und condom perhaps?"

She stopped cold in her tracks. Everyone else, including me, kept dancing. "Can't you be spontaneous ever?" she asked in no accent, shoulders slumped.

"I'm happy to oblige—even eager," I said happily and eagerly. "I'm just not ready for a baby yet."

She shook her head, but I didn't stop dancing. Soon she got into the beat again and she moved close and whispered in my ear. "Do you know how they get sperm from a dead person?" she asked.

"No. I don't particularly want to know. I suppose they have to cut into the body."

She smiled. "It's easier than that," she said. "I found out today that they just take a cattle prod-like thing, stick it up his butt, and give a jolt of electricity. It makes the dead ejaculate."

"Gross!" I yelled. "Please, I don't like hearing that kind of stuff."

"That's how those parents harvested sperm from their dead son. They'll be grandparents."

I didn't even want to think about it. It must have shown on my face because she laughed. Then she became all sexy again, dancing. After awhile she said, "Maybe I should get the device to use it on you—one way to get your sperm."

Now I stopped cold. "I know you want a baby, okay? And we will. Tonight is just not the night." I whipped off the dance floor onto the walled-in porch. I was too hot now. Kathleen followed.

"Hugh, it's like you have Asperger's Syndrome when it comes to the finer art of wooing."

"I woo plenty fine. I must have done something right to marry you." I thought of how we wed on the beach and had my good friend the mime officiate.

"Woo woo," she said.

"Are you trying to get my goat?"

"If you had a goat, its milk would be sour."

"What's that mean?"

"You'd understand if you knew women—too bad you had no sisters."

"And I went to a boys' school, too."

"Exactly. Those were critical years," she said. She turned away. "I'm going to get something to eat. Maybe a cream pie," and she turned on her heel. She left with her syllables biting into me.

"You go do that," I replied. I stayed on the porch and I watched my corpse bride in white, gray around the edges, walk off. The sea of people parted in front of her.

What was I supposed to do now? Out there on the porch, I looked through the front door at the strange dancing people. A giant yellow mustard bottle spun with her husband dressed as a hot dog. There was a Girl Scout in a short slutty skirt whose troop number was 69, and she danced with a bearded man as a giant mint cookie. Perhaps their childish behavior and carefree attitude was merely a respite from their more complex lives with bosses berating them, spouses misunderstanding them, and the world chewing into their hides. Why not dance? We're merely blobs of water and minerals procreating to create what? It was a world run over with gas-guzzlers and pollution and cattle prods for semen.

The music changed to the Rolling Stones' "Sympathy for the Devil," and cheers went up. In a swirl of masks and mania, everyone danced that much harder. I grabbed the digital camera around my neck. The scene spoke to me, like angels to Abraham, and I needed that picture. The light was low, though. According to my meter, one-fifteenth of a second was needed, s long for a clear shot. I had to steady myself. If I ɟainst the wall and held my breath, I might get it. I ɫeaned back, but the wall must have been farther back than I had anticipated because I didn't feel it, which caused me to trip, and I was falling, tipping back. I realized in a horrible instant that the wall was not solid but merely cloth, designed with a brick motif. I fell backwards from the front porch. Dracula soared into the night.

They say time slows down when you're in a very dangerous moment, and it's true. Above me, I saw a rising tower of bones, and, beyond that, stars in the sky. I felt extraordinarily alone, and I knew right then where I was. I was falling underneath the giant skeleton into the garden. I pictured myself plunging down five feet in an arc that any engineer could have plotted. Oops.

Then I heard a lot of crunching sounds like a wood crate breaking. Was that me? I couldn't breathe and felt searing pain. I looked up. The giant skeleton shook and cracked. I must have hit one of its legs. Bones like arrows shot toward me. While I couldn't breathe, I still covered my head. We are creatures designed for survival. Miraculously, with thudding around me, no bone hit me.

Then I thought: I may be dying anyway.

Then I thought: this is it. Death—it's too damn simple.

Then I thought: I'll never see Kathleen again. That made me sad.

And I was desperate for air.

I could feel air.

I could feel air coming in. A little. I uncovered my eyes and saw a man. He wore leather S & M straps. "Can you talk? Hello?" he said. I couldn't. I was still trying to catch my breath, and my back was on fire. Even so, I had a strange thought: this is someone I wouldn't normally talk to.

Another person spoke, and I turned to see the hot dog. "Should we call 911?" said the man as a wiener and bun.

"I— I— can breathe," I managed. "Maybe... if you... could you... lift me to my feet?" My breathing was short.

"Should we call the ambulance?" said Mr. S & M while I remained on my back.

"Maybe we should get him a board," said the hot dog, "for his back."

By now other people had gathered around me, clearing away bones. The circle included a boxer in a fake muscle suit and a woman in black with white dashes down her middle. She had an Interstate shield painted on one of her abundant breasts. "Who are you?" I gasped.

"The 405 Freeway," she said.

"Please lift me up," I asked.

The men lifted, and I stood on shaky legs.

"Look at his back," said somebody. "Lift up the black table-cloth."

"It's a cape," I said weakly.

"Pretty bloody," said another. Doesn't look good."

The 405 Freeway pulled something that seemed caught in the top of my pants. She held before me a broken sprinkler head on top of a long white broken PVC pipe.

"It really scraped up your back, cut a hole in your shirt, too," said the hot dog. "Otherwise, you're probably okay."

"Lucky the pipe wasn't copper or it'd be through him," said Mr. S & M.

Where was Kathleen? I needed her more than ever. A re-frigerator-sized guy dressed as a security man waddled in. "Security" was emblazoned in yellow across his black coat. Then I remembered he was a real security man, one of two in charge of checking people into the party. He looked so big and serious, I automatically said, "I'm fine. Really, I didn't drink that much—it's a fake wall." I pointed. It was then I saw my hand was cut up and bloody, too. My hand had shot out thanks to my wonderful autonomic nervous system. My hand had helped break my fall, assisting the sprinkler head in doing the same thing. Hence, my head hadn't hit the ground.

At this point, my Corpse Bride ran over.

"I just heard," she said. "Are you okay?" She looked aghast. I nodded. She said, "Someone ran in and said my husband had fallen. I'd seen people out here a minute earlier, but I thought it was a drunk in the bushes."

"No, it was me, Dracula."

We kissed. We kissed hard.

Randolph rushed in, still holding his club. "Are you all right, mate? Are you all right?" he asked. Did he have an Australian accent now?

"I've been better," I said.

"Oh, mercy," he replied, looking out at his field of bones. He turned back to me, refocused. "Let's get you cleaned up," he said. He and Kathleen led me into the kitchen.

Just beyond the doorway of the kitchen, a woman dressed in short vinyl shorts and a vinyl bra, rings in her lip, nose, and eyebrow, and deep dark makeup ate pie.

She looked at me, impressed. "Halloween blood," she said as a statement.

"No, real blood," I said.

"Even better," she replied.

Kathleen and Randolph shuttled me toward the sink.

"My first aid kit's in here," said Randolph. "Face your wife," he said. I held Kathleen's hand. She still looked worried. My breathing was a little better. "Here we go," said Randolph.

The first sensation was a cool towel then a deep sting as if he were shoving a stake into my heart from behind. "Yeooowwww!" I screamed. "What the hell are you doing?"

"Rubbing alcohol kills all germs," he said. The pain was enough to make my reflection disappear from the mirror.

"Oh, your hand," said Randolph, taking it, and before I could protest, he pushed an alcohol-soaked paper towel onto my hand, and it felt like a hundred nails. Dracula was being crucified.

"Time to go home?" said Kathleen.

"Please," I said. I'd been too alone without her.

As we walked through the dance floor, the man whose head was inside a fish tank said, "Are you all right?"

"I had fun," I mumbled. "It was as good as jamming bamboo shoots under my fingernails."

We walked slowly to the car, past the bones on the lawn, past the graves, past the two chunky security guards at the head of the driveway. They were having a smoke and looked at my hunched figure slinking into the night. Kathleen held my hand, guiding me.

When we turned the corner onto the main street, the stream of cars was only binocular lights to me. It then occurred to me: we had to cross that street, and I was dressed completely in black: black pants, black shoes, black socks, and, of course, a black shirt and cape, both with holes in them as large as the hole in my confidence. My life was in danger before and now again. I couldn't escape.

Kathleen squeezed my hand as if knowing all this. She held out her other hand in front of her like an assured traffic cop. The traffic stopped. We crossed and no one honked.

We were safe. I saw our car. As I gingerly dug for the car keys in my pocket with my sore hand, I gazed at Kathleen who looked at me not as crazy or inept but with concern. It was as if we were two souls with telepathy.

The whole evening rushed at me: my stubbornness, our fight, and my sudden fall as I plunged toward death alone. I could have died, one of those stupid ain't-it-weird deaths in a two-inch column in the newspaper. But I wasn't dead, and I wasn't alone. As sore as I was, I felt extraordinarily lucky—and luckier as I looked at Kathleen and grinned. She returned the gesture, smiling like the open sea. I laughed, and she opened her arms to welcome me. We danced in an embrace to the music still audible a block away, the Stones' "Sympathy for the Devil."

And I thought: it's as if by lightning we're born, and by its thunder we're gone. What the hell was I waiting for?

The two houses next to us had their lights completely out, and in the large gap between the houses, the lawn led to a grouping of pines, a small forest. I took Kathleen's hand and led her to a soft grassy spot by a bush and, standing, kissed her madly. She kissed back with fervor, needing me as much as I needed her. In moments, we tore at each other's clothes, discarding them like hermit crabs their shells. Despite my injuries, the pain faded. Naked and kissing, we moved slowly to our knees, and soon I felt soft moss under my back. Kathleen lay on me, her soft weight melting into me. We made love.

Afterwards, side-by-side on our backs and close, we watched through the trees the moon appear. It was the tiniest of crescents. What I didn't know then was that I had cracked a rib in my fall. What I also didn't know was that in two days I would happen to cough, which would separate my rib into two, sending me into such a white-walled paroxysm of pain that I'd have to be ambulanced from my work's law library to a hospital. What I *did* know now, however, wedged there against the warmth of Kathleen, was that she was quietly laughing, happy, and I knew why. If we had created a baby, then perhaps he or she had been sparked to life by our closeness and joy. Someone could carry that on.

The traffic swished by. We peered upwards, flat and still at the celebration of stars.

The Farms at 93rd and Broadway

One New York night, Hubert Parwinkle turned to his wife Edith, who was reading the Sunday *Times* with him, and said, "You ain't bad."

She laughed, then looked at him, puzzled, "What made you say that?"

"I'm thinking," said Hubert, "that here we are. Kids're grown, out of college, doing well and—"

"Even Sarah."

"Yes. Whoever expected her to find money in acting?"

"I did," said Edith.

"Anyway, Gordon is married and—"

"I don't understand."

"Can't you not cut me off all the time? In twenty-eight years—"

"Thirty next month. Can't you get to the point?"

"Never mind," he said. He rattled his newspaper, the business section, and returned to reading about the possibility of change happening again in the prime rate.

"I'm sorry," Edith said. "I'm listening."

He looked up from his paper. She leaned toward him, her wavy shoulder-length gray hair falling forward. Her attentiveness for a second reminded him of when they were in their twenties. "Things just felt right there for a moment," he said. "We're reading the paper, and I glanced at you, and you looked content. That made me think how we've had our ups and downs, but now we have our coffee and the *Times* together. We're all right."

"Yes, you're right," she said. "We are. And I love you, too."

He wasn't talking about love. She didn't understand. Love's a good thing, yes, and that's probably what he should have said, but that wasn't his point. He was about to say something to clarify, but she was already back to reading, focused on the arts section. She put her finger on the page, reading more closely.

"Did you hear about this?" she asked. "Twenty at twenty? For two weeks, tickets for a number of Off-Broadway shows can be purchased for just twenty dollars, twenty minutes before show time." She looked up. "Doesn't that sound like fun? Do you want to go—in celebration of what you just said?"

He laughed without thinking. There she was, taking his words and using them incorrectly again. She frowned, and he caught himself. What did he want here—to prove a point or let it go? Maybe going out would make her happy and feel cared for. It was good to feel cared for.

He looked at his Rolex. It was just after five. "Sure, why not?" he said. "Tonight?" This is what he liked about these days where responsibilities had lessened, yet they had a good income, far better than they had had in college.

She smiled wide. "Yeah. What do you want to see?" She handed him the list.

He scanned the list of nearly thirty plays. Only one did he know anything about, one that had been running forever. "How about *The Fantasticks?*"

"Really? That's the first play we ever saw together. Remember?" she said, looking off as if trying to recall when life was so tender and love was an ember about to billow.

"You liked it, right?" he asked.

She nodded. "*The Fantasticks* it is. You're very romantic tonight. I like that."

He smiled as if that were his intention. Maybe they'd roll in the hay. Now that her menopause thing was mostly over, she was actually more affectionate these days than she had been for years. You wait long enough, things can happen.

They left their penthouse, took the elevator down, and ate at the vegetarian place at 93rd and Broadway—near where they lived. They grabbed the subway at 96th, exited at 50th Street, and walked less than a block to the theatre. He and Edith had lived once in New Jersey in a house on a beautifully wooded street at the end of a cul-de-sac. They'd purchased the home after they'd sold their first co-op at a ridiculously high price. New Jersey, though, didn't have this—the heartbeat of culture. They'd moved back to the city.

Now thirty-five minutes before show time, ready to stand in a line, they found no line. Hadn't other people seen the announcement in the paper? A man read a newspaper behind the counter. "Where is everyone?" asked Hubert.

"Tuesday nights, the show starts at seven. You've missed almost half an hour. Want tickets anyway?"

Hubert blinked, trying to understand. "Why would you have a curtain time at seven? That doesn't make sense."

"It's their play, dear," said Edith. "They can—"

"I know it's their play!" said Hubert, swinging around. "Did I ask you if it was their play? If I were an investor, I'd want to maximize the number of—"

"It has to do with getting enough sleep," said the ticket man. "The cast has a matinee performance on Wednesdays."

"See, there's a reason," said Hubert to his wife.

Edith glared at him, always her trick. He glared right back.

"I'm sorry," she said at last. She left it at that.

"So which play do you want to see instead?" he asked. Because she'd apologized, he'd let her have the next choice. "We can walk fast to another theatre. Do you have the list?"

"I thought you had the list," she said.

"Why would I have the list?"

"There's a great comedy show next door," said the ticket guy. "Robert White's a stage hypnotist. Only twenty bucks these next two weeks, and he's funny."

"We could use some comedy," said Edith.

"And why could we use a comedy?"

Edith said nothing.

Hubert looked back at the ticket man. "Aren't there any good dramas around?"

"A sure thing next door," said the ticket guy. "White's funny."

Hubert sighed. "Edith, you know hypnotists. They make people act like chickens."

"He's funnier than that," said the ticket guy.

Hubert held out his hand to Edith. "If you think we need comedy, let's go."

They found a long line next door, but it was moving. It was twenty minutes before the show. By the time they bought their tickets, however, the place was nearly full. The only seats left were in the front row. Hubert wasn't a fan of sitting close to a comedian. He and Edith had once seen David Letterman in the front row at a comedy club, and Letterman kept making fun of Hubert's jacket, all suede leather. "It's better than chiffon, right? Chiffon crinkles," Letterman had said. It'd been the late seventies—what did Letterman have against leather?

"There, honey," said Edith. "In the front row."

They sat in the front row. They had no choice.

Mr. White came onstage a few minutes after eight, wearing a black sports coat, a black shirt, and a black tie as if he were in the Mafia. He kept bowing humbly at the applause he received. Behind him, a curtain rose, revealing fifteen straight-backed chairs. Hubert wasn't clapping, but Edith was, and she elbowed him. He wasn't going to clap for someone who hadn't done anything yet.

"Thank you," said Mr. White, who then approached the elevated stage's edge. Looking down at Hubert, he said, "I couldn't help but notice you, sir. I was just like you when I was in high school science class." Mr. White crossed his arms and looked out in exaggerated skepticism. "Oh, yeah?" he said in a deep voice. "Prove it to me."

The audience burst out laughing.

"I'm going to need fifteen volunteers." People raised their hands. White turned back to Hubert and pointed. "Sir, would you like to be one of them?" Hubert shook his head.

"I didn't think so," said Mr. White, "but that's okay. I need to prove it to you first. Volunteers. Please raise your hands if you'd like to volunteer."

Edith raised her hand enthusiastically. Many others around them did, too. Why would anyone want to be humiliated in front of others? "Put your hand down," said Hubert. "You don't want to be a spectacle."

She glared at Hubert and wiggled her arm and hand that much harder. Was this how a matronly mother of two should be acting? This made Hubert consider walking out right then and there. Edith would be mad at him for weeks, though, if he abandoned her.

Mr. White began selecting people. "You, and you," he pointed and bypassed Edith. "If I've selected you, please take a chair onstage." He walked into the aisle with his wireless microphone and picked others, then returned as the final audience members took their seats onstage.

"Why would you want to go up there?" whispered Hubert to Edith as if he'd just witnessed a drunk person pondering crossing a busy street against the light.

"Can't you have a little fun?" she said. "You're turning into an old man."

"Somehow I miscounted," Mr. White said, pointing to an empty chair. "Who else wants to come up?"

Edith leaped out of her chair, arm raised, and Mr. White laughed. "Okay, you're lively," and as she came onstage, he asked, "Are you related to the skeptical gentleman?"

"I'm his wife," she said into the offered microphone. "I'm Edith."

"But you're not a dingbat, right?"

The audience laughed. Clearly they were old enough to know the television show *All in the Family* that he'd referenced.

"No, and my husband's no Archie Bunker—I hope. He's a dentist."

Several guffaws burst out, and Hubert cranked himself around. Who thought dentistry funny?

"And fine teeth you have." More people laughed, and Edith took the last chair.

Hubert wished that those who laughed would break a tooth. Let's see who they'd call then.

"Okay, I'm going to hypnotize you as a group," said Mr. White to those seated on stage. "We're going to have a relationship here, and as in all relationships, it can get odd."

People onstage laughed, some nervously.

"Before I start, let me explain." He turned back to the audience. "The human mind is a powerful thing. Consider all the weird things we do as human beings. How many of you knock on wood or have lucky numbers, or some of you don't step on cracks in case you might break your mother's back?"

A number of people clapped and laughed. Hubert stewed.

"It's as if such magical thinking truly has effect, right? I yell at the sportcasters on TV as if they can hear me. 'Go, go, go!' If I cheer loud enough, too, my team might win."

A number of men laughed. Hubert cracked a smile.

"How about obsessive-compulsive behavior, hear of that? Some people wash their hands thirty, forty times a day. Their mind makes them do it. That's strange, you think, but comedian David Sedaris as a kid had a compulsion to lick light switches and make high-pitched noises."

People laughed. Hubert nodded. One of his hygienists once had to knock on the walls as she walked.

"Then there's rationalization, our way of talking ourselves into something. People rationalize away such things as being mean to a coworker or putting down someone of a different country or religion. It's okay, we tell ourselves. They're not like us. The power of the mind. We invade Iraq offensively, calling it defense. Then people there strap on bombs and kill civilians, calling it good. They'll get seventy virgins or something in heaven, right? The power of the mind."

Hubert nodded more. No one in the audience said a word. This guy was right, though.

"The Irish Catholics and the Irish Protestants—both believing in Jesus Christ and turning the other cheek, each sharing the same ethnicity and culture, killed each other for years in the name of their religions. Sometimes I think if we didn't have rationalization, we'd be a better world. "

Hubert clapped with others.

Mr. White turned around and walked back to the volunteers on stage. "Ladies and gentlemen, I'm pointing out the power of the human mind, and your minds are amazing things, as you'll see. I'm going to put you under and then ask you to do things. People may laugh, but pay it no mind. Just listen to me. Put your hands in your lap facing upwards. Please close your eyes and listen."

Edith and the volunteers did as he suggested. The lights dimmed and gentle piano music played over the PA. Mr. White spoke softly, pleasantly, telling them to allow themselves to let go, feel deeply relaxed. "Breathe deeply. Focus on your facial muscles and feel each one at ease.

"Let the hands rest in the lap and relax," said Mr. White. "Feel your hands at ease. Make them float as if on a cloud. Feel at peace. You are at peace. Relax. Imagine a babbling brook in the woods, and you're hearing those peaceful sounds. Relaxing feels so good, doesn't it? Allow yourself to relax. Allow yourself the peace you need, you want."

The piano started sounding like the rhythm of a brook. Hubert himself felt at peace listening to this.

"That's it, good, you're doing it. When I snap my fingers, allow yourself to go limp, but don't open your eyes. I'll count to three and snap my fingers. Then you'll go limp. Ready?"

He counted and snapped his fingers. The lights snapped on more brightly, and everyone on stage went limp, including Edith, who fell over into the lap of her neighbor. People laughed. Hubert leaned forward, raised his hand, concerned.

Not noticing Hubert, Mr. White hurried over to Edith. "Sit up, dear. You're okay." He helped her back up. "You're fine, just sit up."

Hubert sat back. At least Mr. White cared.

The music of *The Nutcracker Suite* started, and Mr. White said, "Feel this music. If you want to get up, open your eyes, and dance to it as your favorite ballet artist, go ahead. Dance in your seat. Do what you want to do."

A skinny man started conducting with an imaginary baton. Others kept their eyes closed and moved their arms and legs. Two older men arose, one portly, one bald, eyes open, and started tip-tip-tip-toeing as if in a tutu in a ballet. Many people were laughing. Edith stood and pirouetted, flinging her arms out of rhythm. "Look at that woman!" someone said, laughing hard. This Hubert didn't like. "Stop it," he shouted to his wife beneath the din. "Edith, please sit down."

The music changed to "76 Trombones" from *The Music Man*. "All right, volunteers," said Mr. White. "When I snap my fingers on three, I want you all to become your favorite person or animal. Be the person or animal you most like when I snap my fingers. Ready?"

He counted and snapped his fingers. The volunteers instantly changed—all except the man who had been conducting; he was still conducting. The portly man was now strolling like a man deep in thought. "E equals MC squared," he said. The bald man was an elephant swinging one arm as a trunk. Edith shouted "buck buck buck" and walked like a chicken.

Hubert grimaced. She was doing this to mock him.

A younger man, well-built and looking a bit like Tom Cruise, strutted like her, hands on his waist and swinging his elbows out like wings. He shouted, "Cock a doodle do!" Edith saw him, smiled and strutted around him flirtingly. The audience laughed uproariously.

"Edith," shouted Hubert.

The young man got behind Edith and tried mounting her. The roar of the audience rose. "Hey!" shouted Hubert. "Edith! Goddamn it, you're not a chicken. Edith, stop that. That's disgusting. You are not a chicken."

Edith stopped. She looked around baffled, then saw the rooster behind her babbling "buck buck buck," and she looked embarrassed. People were laughing even harder at this, and Mr. White, only now seeing what was happening, ran over to her. He whispered in her ear. She nodded, thanked him, and walked toward the stairs off of the stage.

As she was taking her seat next to Hubert, and as people were laughing at what was still happening onstage, Hubert looked at her sternly. "You made an absolute fool out of yourself. Happy?"

"As a matter of fact," she said. "I was. You're really stuffy. In your previous life, I think you were a jackalope."

"There's no such thing as a jackalope," he said. "That was just a stupid card we saw at Stuckey's."

"Then you were a grinch."

He was ready to say there were no such things as grinches either, but she'd burst up from her chair and started striding up the aisle, out of the theatre. "Edith," he said, following desperately, which only made those nearby laugh at that, too.

Behind him, Mr. White said, "Sir, sir? Did I prove it to you?"

The audience erupted, and if humiliation could be water, Hubert was under a tidal wave.

When he caught up with Edith outside the theatre, he said, "Come on, now. I'm on your side."

"I saw your face," she said.

"I was concerned. I only want the best for you."

She continued walking quickly toward the subway entrance. "Yes, best like an SS officer wants the best."

"That's unfair," he said. "That's completely unfair to use the Holocaust in anything."

"You're not fair."

He kept quiet as they pushed the rest of the way to the subway. She had her own Metro card, and he anticipated she wasn't going to let him use it as she had on the way to the theatre. Indeed, she ran her card at the turnstile, stepped through, and didn't look back. He quickly grabbed his wallet and found his own card.

Once they were on a train going back, holding a pole because the train was so crowded, he whispered, "So you were having a good time onstage, was that it?"

"Yes, I was. I felt relaxed. I was enjoying being there, whatever I was doing."

"You were acting like a chicken."

"I like chickens," she said plainly. "In a previous life, I was a chicken."

Hubert gasped, then saw a seated older woman's mouth fall open. "Mind your business, all right?" he told the lady. "We're rehearsing a play, *My Life as a Chicken*." He turned back to Edith and said, "Ix-nay the Ikin-chay."

"You're sweeping me off my feet with Pig Latin?"

"What do you want?"

"You have a narrow little mind, Hubert. And we have a narrow little marriage, which I'm starting to rethink."

Hubert turned to the woman again, "A powerful line, don't you think?" He returned to Edith and said, "Just stop it."

She made no reply. Back home, striding through the front door, she announced, "I'm going to bed."

"Me, too. That's what we do this time of night."

"Maybe you should sleep in the guest bedroom tonight."

"For what? For being concerned about your well-being onstage?"

She moved her head chicken-like a few times, turned into the bathroom, and locked the door.

"Criminy," he muttered and grabbed a new set of pajamas. He dressed in the bedroom, used his finger as a toothbrush in the guest bathroom, and crawled into their bed. He wanted to be in bed when she emerged. He had a right to be there.

Hubert listened for her movement in the bathroom. First he heard a scratching sound like fingernails on tile—whatever for? Next, she was opening and closing drawers as if looking for something. Then the water tap ran—and water splashed. She must be washing her face.

The tap cranked off and Edith brushed her teeth. He pictured it, her vigorous brushing up and down creating foam at her mouth. As her dentist, he'd told her dozens of times over the years that that wasn't the best way to brush. She wore out toothbrushes quickly, but instead of listening to his advice, she'd recently found a new dentist, "her own dentist," as she said. Even he said she was a little too vigorous on her gums.

Enough of this crap. No more talking about chickens or previous lives or going to stupid comedy clubs. She needed some rules if this was going to work. They perhaps had twenty to thirty years left together. He realized then that, hell, they might only be at the halfway point of their lives together. Another thirty years?

The door opened. Edith emerged in a black nightgown. He forgot everything. "I didn't know you still had that nightgown," he said. Her breasts beneath the sheer black material swayed. She'd always had well-proportioned breasts.

"This is not what you think. I can hardly have sex with you tonight, now can I?"

"I think you've misunderstood me."

"I just want to feel pretty, and this does it for me."

"But do you even understand me?" he reiterated.

"Does it matter? I'm not the right wife for you. You should have a new wife."

"Or, right, like it's time I go to the wife store or something?"

"I don't care what the hell you do. I'm moving to a farm."

"A farm? You couldn't even take New Jersey."

"I have to return to my roots," she said, getting into bed.

"Your roots? Let me just say here and now—"

"I don't want your bullying anymore. Tonight I remembered my previous life. It all came back. I lived on a farm as a chicken."

"Listen—"

"I was a white chicken," she said seriously. "Don't laugh. Or laugh, I don't care, but I remember the land was flat, and the farmer spoke a guttural language. Maybe it was Danish."

"You were a Danish chicken?"

"Your skepticism is poison—it always has been." She glared at him, grabbed the blankets, and turned away from him.

"I don't see—"

"Please shut up."

"Okay, I'm sorry. I'll listen." He felt stupid saying it, but if it'd make her feel better...

"I remember there was death there."

"Where?" he asked.

"The farm. The pigs squealed most loudly when the farmer took his axe out, and my father, a rooster with a powerful strut, took me to the barn where there was blood in the dirt. I didn't quite understand, but maybe beneath it all, I did."

This was ludicrous. She turned onto her back and stared into the ceiling, perhaps picturing the farm. He realized she believed she'd been a chicken. The hypnotist had done something terrible to her mind. He felt his stomach drop. He needed to help her. How? What if he could get her to Dr. Arkmenian in the morning? They'd go to the clinic. But what if she didn't want to go? Flu shots—they needed flu shots. He could get her to go for that. They had great insurance. Still, he had to do something fast.

"I was a rooster in my previous life," he heard himself saying. It sounded all right. Funny how it'd popped into his head and now he was saying it.

"Stop playing with me," she said. "I'm tired of it."

"I was a rooster," he repeated, "just like your Dad," and he looked off the way she had done. "There were hills on my farm, and it was very green and rainy all the time. Maybe it was Wisconsin. I remember a lot of mud. But it was so green there, I loved it." He could picture just such a place. Maybe he'd been to the farm as a kid.

"A chicken's life is good," she said. "You can run around."

"Yes. And—" He stopped because he pictured a little girl. She had ponytails.

"What?" said Edith.

"A little girl was there, and so was a wheelbarrow that she played with in the yard. That little girl made me her pet. I walked with her everywhere outside, right behind her and that red wheelbarrow." He gasped, and as he did so, he felt a sense of darkness, of something sad. He couldn't tell what at first.

"What?" asked Edith. "What happened?"

The farm was so visible to him at that moment. A man was getting out of a car, a man with a felt hat from a very old car, a Model A perhaps. "A man came to the farm, and he had a bag with him. I don't know how I know this, but he was a doctor. He walked from the car through the mud into the house. There was a light rain outside, but my brothers and sister and I walked near the window to watch. I could see him in the little girl's room with her parents. The doctor stared out the window at us at one point. He shook his head. At that moment—"

He felt a tear rolling down his face. He wiped it, and he could feel himself shake. This was truly crazy—what the hell was his mind doing? Yet he felt so deeply sad.

"What?" asked Edith.

"The little girl died," he said. "I don't know why."

He did not understand what was going on. Was he as insane as Edith? Or did it have to do with needing sleep? He cried as if he had no choice. As he did so, Edith held him under her wing, and she said, "You're all right."

Catalina

Daunus handed his ticket to the man in the crisp white naval-style uniform for the boat to Catalina Island, and the man paused, looking him up and down as if Daunus might be a terrorist. "I'm Greek," said Daunus emphatically with an accent, grabbing his thick half-gray beard and then pointing to his black fishing cap. "And I've been a U.S. citizen seventeen years!"

"I don't doubt you," said the man.

"Want to look in my rucksack?"

"No need. Welcome to Catalina Express."

The pier was higher than the boat, so Daunus stepped down the gangplank toward a sleek 300-passenger catamaran, shaking his head. After all he gave this country, people still looked at him like he didn't belong. This trip was folly. He shouldn't have listened to his friend.

Once on the boat, he marched up the stairs to the top deck, moved past the outside seating area and into the cabin. The airline-style seating inside was nearly full. He didn't want to sit next to anyone, so he returned outside where he found two seats isolated from the others. He placed his green rucksack on the extra seat. No one asked him to remove it. Few people sat outside because it was a cool, gray day.

When the boat backed up then moved forward through the Long Beach channel, a young woman in a red sweater and sunglasses approached him but did not look at him. Rather, she stood at the side near him, looking off toward the front of the boat. What's to see? Gray clouds?

She then turned toward him. "Have you been to Catalina before?" She looked like a movie star with her red lipstick—the kind of person who had people wash her dishes.

"Never," he said, leaving it at that.

"Me neither. Staying long?"

"Just the day. My friend said I needed it."

"Oh?"

"Yeah." A loss for her was probably getting a dent in her Porsche.

"Sorry," she said. "Didn't mean to pry. How cool it's an island, though, huh?"

"My friend said it's like a persimmon—unexpected fruit on a naked tree." He looked at her woefully cheerful face.

"Wow," she said. "I wish I'd said that."

"I shouldn't have listened. I shouldn't be here."

She nodded. "Well, I hope you find your fruit," she said with a movie-star smile and stepped to the other side of the boat.

Once out of the port, the catamaran pushed its engines to full and stabbed into the mist that hung over the dark water. For the full hour-ride, Daunus sat outside, looking rearward into the gray wake. At one point, a white baseball cap landed in the wake. Someone lost it. His chest felt constricted. Breathing was hard. He'd given this country everything, including now his son. Daunus had supported Mr. George W. Bush—even Iraq. What did such devotion do for him? The churned water faded into the horizonless backdrop. Bloody fuckin' America.

Entering Avalon, the only city on Catalina, the boat moved like a dark eel into the cave-like bay, past the silent million-dollar yachts and a tarped black speedboat, all at anchor. The dry hills leaping from the water were like Chora Sfakion in Crete. His friend must have known.

Daunus stood and turned his attention to the shoreline, a narrow dead beach that fronted a line of restaurants and shops with awnings. Because it was midweek in November, the high season had passed, and so there were no eager shoppers or young couples strolling the boulevard as summer days had probably promised. The happy time was over.

With the boat approaching the dock, a crowd headed to the stairs to descend to the first level. Daunus inserted himself in front of a kid and started to feel lightheaded. He was anxious, he supposed. Once off the boat with the crowd, he did his best to stop hyperventilating and felt like an old car shaking apart. One step, then another, he told himself. He moved with everyone toward the town center, passing a shaded grassy area. He came upon bricks arranged in a square. Names and dates were on the bricks and when he caught the word "veterans," he became dizzy and his breathing became shorter, shallower. He pictured his son in uniform, proud and innocent, muscles like a thoroughbred. Daunus grabbed a nearby rail. Was he going to pass out here?

He thought he heard a bird above him, a caw. He paused, raised his head. High above the town, the scrubby hills stood naked, even burned in some places. The yearly autumn Santa Ana winds had sucked all the moisture from every tendril on the rocky soil, and a careless spark from a construction worker had set off a firestorm. As he'd seen on television, hundreds of fire fighters and dozens of fire trucks had been moved by hovercraft from the mainland and saved the town, but the hillsides remained scarred.

The young woman in red walked by and said, "Definitely a persimmon! Isn't this place beautiful?" She gave him another smile, and he realized she was carrying a heavy backpack with a bedroll strapped on. He'd read her completely wrong. She was going camping.

He tipped his cap to her. She nodded appreciatively in return and walked off. Air now filled his lungs easily. Daunus stepped forward more surely. "Go, mister," he told himself with a nod. He knew where he wanted to walk: high into the heavenly white ash.

The Sun
Is a
Billiard
Ball

For the fifth day in a row, when Albert wiped himself on the john, the tissue showed blood. In the first few days, he ignored the color and simply considered that it was not worth thinking about. When he first saw that his underwear had a dark, long, narrow stain, like a line had been drawn with a marker, he told himself it was likely a minor bout with diarrhea. When he felt a trickle as he walked, and he went into a bathroom to check, he could see the leak was definitely red. He hoped it would go away. The body could heal itself. Even so, he took to wearing a kind of sanitary napkin he made of tissue paper. The dots of blood did not stop. And now he swabbed fresh blood.

He sat on the toilet and scratched his face. His thick beard did not feel right. He finished cleaning, made himself another napkin, placed it in his underwear, and pulled up his pants.

He stood in front of the mirror and evaluated himself. For being forty-four, he looked on the outside to be in fairly good shape. He was tall and thin, had very little paunch, and showed muscular arms and shoulders. The Royal Canadian Air Force exercises that his father had taught him had helped—push-ups, sit-ups, scissor jumps, and more. He wondered, though: did he have cancer? As he looked at himself more closely, he saw one thing was off. His dark beard looked a little heavier on one side than the other. He took his orange-handled scissors down from atop his medicine cabinet and trimmed the one side. As he evaluated his work, he felt he had snipped too much. He clipped the other side. Too much again. He trimmed and trimmed and, finally, so angry with himself, he soaked his face under the shower, lathered his face with his wife's shaving cream, and, using her Lady Gillette razor, cut his damn beard off.

He gazed at himself in the mirror. He saw a stranger. His nose, slightly bent from a high school hockey accident, was familiar, as were his probing brown eyes, but his face, which Albert had not seen in almost twenty-three years, seemed to be someone else's. He had not been clean-shaven since his junior year abroad in Amsterdam when he had decided to grow the beard, knowing full well his father hated beards as well as the long shoulder-length hair Albert had grown. In contrast, his father had been bald.

As Albert ran his fingers over his—this stranger's—face, he realized he was already two years older than his father had been when he'd died from prostate cancer. Albert gazed at his own nearly bald head and guessed he had inherited more than just a propensity for a lack of hair. He would likely die the same way his father had. Maybe it was good he had shaved because chemotherapy would make him hairless anyway.

Albert walked past his sleeping wife, Brenda, and past the bedroom of his fifteen-year-old son, and he wondered, who should he tell? His family? Brenda was having her own problems with gallstones and a bad back. This week, in fact, her doctor was going to try to dislodge the latest stone with an ultrasound technique. If it didn't work, it meant surgery. The mid-forties were meant to be fun. Why the hell were he and Brenda so picked on?

Albert opened the front door to get the paper in the exact same ritual he did seven days a week—but the paper was not there on the front porch's tile floor. Instead, his cat, Jennifer, fluffy and old at eighteen years, was licking herself, bent like a stiff contortionist. She looked up at him and stared intently, not blinking or turning away. He stared back. She didn't stop. He knelt down to pet her, but she turned, frightened, and ran off on inflexible legs.

"Jennifer, it's me. Really," Albert called. If the cat had been younger, he thought, her sense of smell, which was now probably gone, would have reassured her. He wondered if he would be dead before his cat—a maudlin thought.

He looked for his newspaper in the driveway and in his garden. The snapdragons were in bloom; their orangeness was fading. He looked behind the plants. The paper was nowhere to be seen.

A high-school student, a young pale woman with a backpack and a lacy bra, which Albert noticed through her translucent white shirt, strode by, glanced at him, saw nothing, and continued on. The world, he sensed in that instant, was going to move on without him.

"Goddamn back," his wife, Brenda, stated as she sauntered out of the bedroom. "I feel like a sack of shit," she said before she really noticed Albert, who was buttering his toast with the new extra light whipped butter. "What the fuck did you do to your face?" she asked. "You look like a billiard ball now."

"Criminy," he let out. Her penchant for the truth had endeared Brenda to him when she'd been twenty-five. She was bleach-haired and wild then, and they were going to fuck like bunnies forever and never marry. Now they drove Volvos, made love once a month if they were lucky, would celebrate their sixteenth wedding anniversary in a week, and her honesty, which was always on high in the morning, was like a garish tattoo.

"I thought you might like this look," Albert said finally.

"Grow it back as fast as you can," she urged while trying to stretch backwards and starting to laugh. "Can't you hide in the bathroom a couple of weeks and then come out?"

"Hey, Dad," Timothy said as he shuffled out of his room in a style not unlike his mother. "Fuck. What the hell happened to you?" Timothy had inherited his mother's word list.

"Can't you two not use foul language for a day?" Albert said. "Why the heck can't a guy just butter his toast and make it through a day as if he didn't live in a truck stop?"

"Gosh darn it, Dad," said Timothy with a grin. "I'll try my blasted best." Albert glared at his son with the green hair and the stud in his cheek. This is where permissiveness had led Albert—to the same disappointed plateau Albert's father must have felt.

"Tim-o-thy," said Albert, running the word's three syllables through his mouth slowly as if the name were as new as the day they named him after Timothy Leary. "Ironic," said Albert, not explaining the thought to his son or puzzled wife. The irony was that his son was as freethinking as Timothy Leary. Also, it occurred to Albert that Leary had died from prostate cancer.

"What the fuck's wrong with him?" Timothy asked, turning to his mother. "And why'd he shave?"

"Fuck it," she said in reply.

Albert, still holding the toast with his left hand, began buttering his toast with too much force, not watching closely. If he had been using a butter knife, nothing would have happened, but the steak knife cut into two knuckles. Blood began to flow.

* * *

That same hour across town, when Jazz awoke in Wade's apartment, she watched Wade sleep. He was like a Michelangelo figure draped with a marble sheet. If she wasn't so close as to see his facial hair, which looked as pointillistic as sandpaper, she indeed might consider him a statue. He was real, though, and his gentleness last night had made her cry.

She glanced around his room and noticed speakers in all four corners and a CD deck with its lights still on. The last Grateful Dead disc must have finished when they had fallen asleep. She took to staring at his ceiling fan turning slowly, feeling as if she were in *Casablanca*. How nice it must have been to live back then. Africa. The war. The enemy was so much more clear then.

Jazz knew Wade was awake when he caressed her breast. "Careful," she said. "They're a little sore from... you know."

"You have such a way with words, Ms. English Major."

"You want me to call you Mr. Window Tinter?"

"I don't mind." He sat up and smiled, twisted left then right to stretch, and stepped out of bed, still nude. With a line of chest hair that marched down his stomach to become the forest of his pubic hair, he looked even more like a statue. He touched his toes. Very limber. Jazz watched as if she were trying to understand a new culture. He ran in place briefly when he caught her gaze.

"Just trying to get my motor running," he laughed.

"Coffee doesn't work?"

"What should we do this morning?" he asked eagerly. "What do you say we run down to Malibu for Eggs Benedict?"

"I don't run anywhere. Are you normally so cheerful when you wake up?"

"Why not? Besides, it's my birthday."

"Really? How old are you?"

"Twenty-six."

"God, I'm robbing the cradle."

"How old are you?"

"Fifty. I just use a lot of baby whale placenta. It was on special this week at the Clinique counter."

"You're in your twenties."

"Thirty-one. And I wasn't a mere undergrad English major, but a doctoral candidate in English. They kicked me out for thinking bad thoughts about James Joyce."

"I like your humor," he said.

"That's one person on earth," she said.

He knelt and lightly kissed her cheek, gentle as a hummingbird. He then drew a finger over and around her breasts. He was definitely a breast man. That's all right. She had worn the silk dress for a reason: her breasts suggested themselves well under it. It was that kind of night. She needed it. She didn't understand how low she had been until Marsha, recently divorced, demanded they go to the Mint on Pico—a club with a rusty sign but a good reputation for music. "Just live a little," Marsha had said.

Many of the women had taken notice of Wade. With his cleft chin, blond hair, and smiling eyes, he looked like one of those handsome actors who peopled soap operas and played the shy but gorgeous friend next door. In a tight T-shirt, black jeans, and leaning against the wall, he had been watching the band. She had forgotten about him until she saw him approach. He asked her to dance.

She touched Wade's face now and was about to say something but stopped.

"What?" he asked, slipping back into bed. He began to rub her shoulders.

She couldn't bring up the one thing on her mind. She passed over it, telling herself she was fine, so what did it matter? She instead said, "You know, if you don't mind my saying so—in the light of day, you're still handsome."

"Maybe once you have coffee, you'll think differently."

"I was trying to imagine what it'd be like to be you, waking up with your face." Her finger skied over his shadow of a beard. "Your skin is perfect, even with all this stubble."

"Who are you to talk? You could be part of *Vogue* or any fashion magazine," he said, "even if your nose is pushed a little to the left."

"Aren't you brimming with compliments," she said.

"A teacher once told me Michelangelo purposely made a single mistake on his artwork because only God could create perfection. You're as perfect as his Pieta."

Jazz laughed. "You pulled your foot out of your mouth. Especially for a..." She let it drop.

"For a window tinter, you mean?"

"You did some fine tinting last night."

Wade offered a little smile, the type given to be kind. He stopped touching her, though, and took to gazing upward toward the ceiling fan, which was on slow. He seemed lost in thought. "What?" she asked leaning on one elbow. "Where are you?"

Rather than respond directly, he reached for her shoulder-length hair.

"I love your red hair," he said, "And, you know, your—"

"I know, my breasts. I had them enlarged last year."

"You did?"

"I love my hair, even love my face," she said, "but my breasts were, you know, a bit small. I'd just turned thirty, I wanted to celebrate, so I bought new breasts."

He leaned slightly and took one breast in his mouth, ran his tongue around her nipple. As she felt her own desire stir, she immediately felt guilty again and pulled away.

"Liar," he said.

Which caught her breath for a second. He couldn't know. "About what?" she said, testing the waters.

"About your breasts. Fake ones are too round, and they don't hang as naturally as yours."

"I guess you've seen a few."

"I'm not bragging."

"You're an attentive lover."

Again he turned away.

"What's wrong?" she asked this time.

"I shouldn't have smoked the joint you had. That made me thirsty, and then I drank, and the combination always does me in. I barely remember how we got here."

"I drove."

"I remember the condom broke, and I kept going. I already have a kid."

"We were both desperate, as I recall."

"Desperate?"

"Needing it," she said. "You have a child?"

"Yeah. A little girl. My girlfriend took off with her, and... I keep thinking I could've done something more." He turned to face her better. "I'm sorry. It's not the kind of thing I should be talking about now. Nothing against you." She saw him look off again, as if his daughter were calling him. He whispered, "Where does trust go in this world?"

She couldn't say.

"I guess she figured a window tinter wasn't going to support her well," he said.

"I'm sorry."

"What the heck, Jazz."

"And I take the pill," she said.

"You didn't say that last night."

"I should say I took the pill up until two weeks ago, but the body doesn't react that fast. You're safe, you're... safe."

"Why'd you stop taking it?" he asked.

"Figured I'd be celibate for a while," she quipped. "Guess it's like putting a picnic blanket out. I invited rain."

He laughed, which broke the tension she'd felt. He leaned in, and she accepted his kiss. Even with their morning breath she didn't mind. It made her feel whole again. Then the thought started hammering at her once more. She gently pushed him away. This wasn't fair to him.

"What?" he said. "I've got different condoms."

The irony was too much. She slipped out of bed, found her pink underpants on the floor and pulled them on quickly. "Work," she said.

"Work? I thought you were a student."

"No. Kicked out, remember? I really need to spend my morning looking for work," she said, scanning the floor. "Where's my bra?"

"Not even breakfast?"

She shook her head.

"How about we just go to the beach? It's so beautiful in the morning—a perfect thing for a birthday."

His face reminded her of her late dog, Seymour, a woolly mongrel with an expression that always showed such hope when she approached the kitchen. How could she turn Wade down, and on his birthday? All she could say, though, was, "My bra?"

He leapt out of bed and, with his foot, pulled her bra out from under his rocking chair by his stereo. He flicked the garment to her with such a smile on his face, she felt saddened she would not be able to see him again.

"I'm sorry," she said. "No beach for me today."

She turned her back to him as she pulled on her bra. She could tell he was watching, and it made her feel more naked than she was. She lifted her breasts to accommodate the bra.

"I've always wondered what it must be like to go around with breasts," he said.

She laughed. "You know, I've always wondered that about men. They walk around with this big thing in their crotch. It flops this way or that, and if they get, you know, excited, it gets hard and obvious. Seems like it could be embarrassing at times."

"It is," he said.

"Can you hand me my dress?" she asked.

Standing, he used his toes to grab her dark silk dress from the floor as if he were on a high wire, the Great Wallenda. She stepped into her dress, slipped on her black heels, and grabbed her black purse from the chair. She hadn't had to wear the same clothes the next day for years. Doing so made her feel oddly young. She bounced toward the door.

"I directed a play," he said. "Would you like to go see it?"

She turned. "A play?"

"Yeah. *The Imaginary Invalid*—a comedy. I window tint to support myself in theatre. I really think the magic's in theatre."

Magic. How she wished she believed in magic. "We can't see each other again," she said, "I'm sorry."

"You're married?"

She let the moment hang. She shook her head. "No." She traced his face again with her eyes.

"Did I do something wrong?" he said, pulling on white underwear. "If I did, I apologize."

"No. You were fine... I'm sorry. Someone as handsome as you must have new girlfriends every week."

"I'm glad you think so, but I'm not that way. Why can't we see each other?"

"I'm sorry."

"You keep saying that."

He looked at her so honestly. So trusting. God. She knew what she had to do. She took a deep breath and moved to his rocking chair, where she sat.

"I had a boyfriend. My so-called boyfriend," she began. "Billy, we'll call him. A cop. He really liked my boobs, too. Apparently he likes not just boobs, though."

"Huh?"

"He's bisexual. I didn't know. He just told me he's HIV positive. He's known for a year.... We've lived together for a year."

"What?" Wade appeared instantly blanched. He moved backwards, found the bed. "I— I—" he began. "Have you been tested yourself?"

"Not yet."

"But even so, you knew you might be..." The silence finished the end of the sentence. He continued, "And you didn't warn— I mean how could you go to a club dressed like that, knowing you might have AIDS? You wore that dress and we danced. You told me you wanted me and—"

"I didn't plan this. I didn't assume this!"

"Yes, you did! You even just said you knew the score."

"I just wanted to be normal for one night. That's not asking too much. Neither one of us wanted the condom to tear."

"You're a loaded gun and you shot me!"

"It was an accident. Accidents happen."

"No such thing."

"It's not all my responsibility."

"It is, Jazz, if that's really your name!"

"Why wouldn't it be my name? You want to see my driver's license?" She opened her black purse and started rummaging through it. "See," she said, holding up her California license with a picture as dorky as in any yearbook. "My name is Jazz Williams."

He lay back on the bed. She didn't move. He didn't either. The overhead fan spun.

* * *

"Gee, Dad," Timothy said before Albert went to work. "Your head kind of looks like a giant egg." As if that weren't enough, he added, "There's more hair on my leftover steak in the refrigerator than anywhere above your shoulders."

"Funny, ha ha," Albert said dryly as Brenda bandaged his two knuckles with Winnie-the-Pooh Band-Aids, years old, the only ones they had in the house.

"Just trying to show you the humor of the situation, Dad," said Timothy, who reached for the Pop-Tarts in the tall cabinet. He ripped a foil pack open, took the two frosted rectangles out, and bit into them together, untoasted.

"Don't be late for school," is all Albert said before heading for his Volvo dealership in Santa Monica. He did not tell Timothy or Brenda about his condition.

Once at work, he waved off his new saleswoman, Carol, with his bandaged hand, as well as Jamie and everyone else who noticed he was clean-shaven. They were either laughing or trying to ask about his new look. Stan, more serious, pulled Albert aside and said he had something urgent to discuss. Albert told all of them, including his secretary, that he just needed fifteen minutes alone. He closed his ornate wooden door that had been carved from Swedish pine in Upsala and sat in his ergonomic executive leather chair. He called his medical group, the HMO near St. John's Hospital, several blocks from his dealership, and he had to describe his symptoms to the woman who answered his doctor's phone.

"In my buttocks—my rectum, I should say," he told the woman. "For five days."

The woman asked if he had had sex using his rectum.

"Of course not!" Albert said. "I run a Volvo dealership!"

"Does it hurt when you walk?" she asked.

As a matter of fact, it did. "This morning, I felt pain as I walked." He didn't offer that it made him waddle funny, which added to the spectacle of being without a beard or of having a bear on his Band-Aids. With such a question, he knew she knew something. "What's that mean?" he said.

"I can fit you in at three today," was her reply. "Can you make it?"

"Yes. Of course."

Brenda called him after he'd hung up to say he hadn't said goodbye before he left. He apologized. "Anything wrong?" she asked.

"Nothing that growing my beard in the bathroom won't solve."

"Come on," she said. "That was a joke. You're a very handsome, older bald guy without wrinkles whose real face we'll all have to get used to."

"Is that supposed to be a compliment?"

"Certainly. Fuck, there's something wrong, and you're not telling me."

"I'm fine, really. Stan probably just sold the used 850R. He's dying to speak to me, so the world is well."

"I'll let you go then. I love you," she said.

"Okay," he said and hung up.

He couldn't keep Stan waiting. Stan was his best salesman, been with him for twelve years. Stan was the only other bearded man on the team, outgoing, friendly, and utterly charming, which is what made him the top salesman. He would surely joke about the death of Albert's beard. Albert wasn't up for more jokes, but he'd have to take them.

Albert buzzed his secretary. "Show Stan in, will you?" he said.

Moments later, the door opened as if Stan had been standing by it. He spoke as he walked, gesturing already with his hands like a politician. "Albert, I like your face, hope you're happy with it. Happiness is a large part of what we all do, surely you agree, and so I'm moving over to a place a little closer to my house. I'll be happier there. Okay? Is that fine? No hard feelings?"

This onslaught of words caught Albert off guard. "What do you mean you're moving closer to your house? You're buying a second house?"

"I'm talking position, work. I'm moving to another dealership."

"What dealership? The only one closer to your place is Mercedes."

"Exactly." Stan then sat, apparently relieved.

"You're leaving Volvo for the Krauts? What, why? We're happy here."

"I have been, yes, but we all change, right? You have your new face, for instance—not that that buys happiness—I tried it once, believe me—but clearly you're a man who's unhappy and you've— Let me say simply it's time I moved on."

"I've what?" said Albert. "I've done something to you? Tell me. I don't want you to go."

"You've been a great guy. Who am I to complain? I'm not like these young kids you brought in to increase the sales force. I don't sell as if people are wallets. I sell because I like to. I sell because Volvos are the safest, best cars around. That and Mercedes."

"The young people are getting to you, is that it?"

"As a friend, Albert, I speak to you. We all know Alex at Mercedes. He approached me, pointed out that his cars aren't cut to the bone in price as the cars here."

"We sell more than they do."

"Yes, but we're all getting just minimums on commissions. What's the point?"

"I sign your paycheck. You're not hurting."

Stan leaned back and laughed. "Let me put it this way. You're so anal these days."

Albert winced. "What do you mean?"

"You're hard on our schedules, hard on our perks. I used to wake up excited to sell here, and we all did better then. It's like a business now, an accounting business. Has it been worth it? You can't tell me your profits are higher than ever."

Stan was right. Profits had taken a deep dive, even though the number of cars sold was up. Volvo was pleased and was sending him and Brenda on an all-expense-paid trip to Gothenburg, Sweden. That certainly didn't make up for the million he'd probably lost. But did either matter now?

"Stan, Stan," Albert said.

"What?"

"I'll miss you."

"And?"

"And what?"

"You'll miss me? That's it? You're not even going to try to talk me into staying?"

"I'm not sure what you want."

Stan rose, incredulous. "Twelve years, and this is all. Christ, I'm glad I'm leaving. What happened to your personality, Albert? What happened to your sales talent and instinct? Something's going on with you and has been for months."

"For months?"

"Yeah. You've gotten more formal, more cold. More Germanic. Maybe you should be the one selling Mercedes."

"I'm— I've—" Albert fumbled for words and looked to his schedule book for an excuse, any excuse. "I was supposed to call Mrs. DuMont at nine. Can we talk later, Stan, after I come back from my doctor's appointment which is at three?"

"You okay?"

"Yeah. A physical. A minor thing."

"Okay, we'll talk later. I like you, you know that. No hard feelings."

"Right. Later."

Stan left, and Albert sighed. His stomach now had pain, worse than when he'd eat at the Chinese place down the street. He loved that stuff, but it always gave him gas. Maybe the cancer was spreading. That made him think how he wanted to leave Brenda and Timothy with a viable company when he died.

What kind of company would it be with his best salesman gone? He should have fought for him.

Albert gazed upon the little toy Volvo 1800 on his desk, given to him months before by a company rep. It was a red car just like the one in the sixties television show, *The Saint*. Albert moved it, and it rolled. He had never noticed it could move. He tried one of the little doors, and it opened. So did the hood. Isn't that funny; some little toy maker in Sweden actually made a tiny replica with working parts.

Albert rolled the car across his latest sales papers and up to a three-ring binder. "Brrrrrr," he said, supplying the sound to the car in the way he had when he was a kid. Albert looked up to see his secretary, Sarah, peeking in through the window at the side. She hurried off.

Albert rolled the toy car to the edge of his desk and let it crash onto the Berber carpet. The doors and the hood popped right off the toy. "Boom," said Albert.

* * *

Wade waited two weeks to make sure the virus, if he had it, could make enough tell-tale signs in his blood. He didn't ask anyone if that's how it worked, but it made sense to him. He wasn't going to be afraid to be tested, as his Uncle Ron had been. As Uncle Ron had become progressively thinner, he had gone to more and more faith healers, acupuncturists, astrologers and health food stores, as if they together held the patent on a long life. Uncle Ron died after weeks in a coma, down to 85 pounds.

On the morning before the test, Wade threw up. The Taco Bell breakfast burrito he had eaten an hour earlier came up, sour. He rinsed his mouth, called information, and asked for the phone number for a Jazz Williams. It was listed. Jazz picked up after the second ring.

"Hello?"

"Jazz, it's me, Wade."

She hung up. He called back. He understood her fear. It wasn't about him.

"Leave me alone!" is how she answered it this time. "I'm sorry about everything, and— I'm just sorry, okay?"

"I'm not calling to harass you or anything," Wade said. "I'm going in for an HIV test at the clinic at St. John's Hospital, and I thought you might like to take the test, too." There was only silence from her end, so he added, "It's better than not knowing, better than this terrible sense that the world is pushing you down more each day. If it's positive, then there are things you can take now that keeps it away. Let's go together."

"I don't know."

"Are you still with the cop?"

"I kicked him out the day he told me."

Good. He had hope. "So can I pick you up?" He heard what he thought was coughing but then realized it was crying. "You okay?"

"You're being so nice. I'm— I'm just sorry about all this."

"Tell me where you live." He could hear the drive in his voice. She shouldn't matter, but she did.

She gave him her address in Santa Monica, a little studio house in the back yard of a bigger house on 17th Street. Twenty minutes later, as he drove there, he wondered why the hell was he doing this? Shouldn't he still be furious? He had to see her. Why? It's the question he gave to his actors. Why are they doing the things they do? They should come up with reasons. Why'd he like Jazz? She had passion. And something else. Darkness. He could help her.

As he passed the Volvo dealership near her house, some sort of commotion was going on in the parking lot between a bald man and another man with a beard. The bald man was holding onto the bearded one as the bearded one tried to pull away. "Stay!" the bald man yelled. The sight made Wade laugh.

Wade parked on Jazz's street and saw a young woman rollerskate down the street wearing short Lycra shorts and a red-white-and-blue-striped bikini top with stars at her nipples. Santa Monica often gave him the feeling he was on one giant movie set, and the people around him were the paid extras.

Jazz opened her door. She wore all brown: blouse, pants, and sunglasses. Wade had to smile. The "incognito" look simply made her appear vulnerable.

"Nice place," he heard himself say. Nice was a word that seemed positive but didn't commit itself to anything, particularly meaning. "Not bad for a student," he added.

"Yeah, well, it's paid for through the first of the month. I wasn't the one paying the rent."

"Your boyfriend did, right? Billy?"

"Yeah. His name is really James, and I hope he dies a long and slow death." She clenched her teeth as if realizing something, and looked to Wade meekly. "I should talk, right? I don't even see how you can look at me again."

"You okay?" he said.

"A bundle of smiles," she said, giving an exaggerated look of terror. In the next instant, she looked at him hard. "Why'd you choose me?"

"Pardon?"

"Why'd you ask me to dance?"

"I liked your face. It had a big question on it."

"Yeah? And now?"

"I'm hoping you'll say yes to another dance."

He motioned toward the street, and they walked, he with his hands in his pockets. Halfway to the car, he felt her take his arm and hold it at the elbow. He didn't expect that. A sense of well-being overcame him. For the remaining steps, time slowed down. The only thing he could compare it to was his first kiss a few days before his fourteenth birthday at summer camp. This was more amazing, though, because it was so unexpected, so unplanned for, and so damn simple. It was just an elbow, yet his penis reacted, and he was having a more difficult time walking. He shouldn't have worn such tight jeans. He had to stop. Her hair in the sunlight was a red corona. Like an angel, he imagined.

"What?" she said.

"My keys." He sorted through one pocket with the arm she did not hold. As he was doing so, he realized that that action brought her to glance at his pocket, not far from his groin. As he often told his actors, movement directs an audience's attention of where to look. If she noticed something, she did not say.

"I hope you don't get sick, Wade, for what I did to you. I'm sorry."

"Yeah." The reminder and the rekindling of fear quickly made him flaccid. In fact, he could barely breathe for a moment, and he felt weak as he opened the car door for her. He said, "I hope you're okay, too."

* * *

Albert drove up and down the streets near Cigna Healthcare, his HMO in an azure blue building, which was three blocks from St. John's Hospital on Wilshire. He searched for parking on the street but could not find any, so he entered the parking structure with apprehension. Ever since the 1994 earthquake caused the parking structure at the Westside Kaiser Hospital to pancake down, he felt as if he were tempting fate by going into such garages. He hated them—but he had to smile. Here he was probably dying of cancer, so what's a few hundred tons of cement? It might be a merciful death. Still, he hoped nothing would happen in this parking garage. He drove all the way to the top. That way there was no ceiling above him.

Just before he turned in, he saw a rollerskater with a red-white-and-blue-striped bikini top. Kids these days. They just play, he thought. Everything is just sex and fun.

Once in the medical building, Albert checked in with the receptionist, who gave him a clipboard that had a form. She also handed him a pen. "Please fill out both sides of the form completely, and then turn it back to me. Both sides, okay?"

"Yes, thanks," said Albert.

He filled out the form, both sides. To the question that said, "Nature of your problem," he wrote the single word "rectum."

A few minutes after he turned in the form, the receptionist said, "Mr. Harris?"

"Yes," said Albert, standing. "I don't understand: rectum? That's not very complete. Are you having a problem around your anus or in your anus or—"

Albert held up his hand, mouth agape. Everyone else in the room—a businessman with a tie, an older woman with white hair, and a man wearing a blue Union 76 shirt—stared at him. Albert quickly stepped closer to the receptionist and whispered, "Can't I just talk to the doctor about this?"

She glared at him and said, "Sentences have a subject and verb, you know. Is your rectum your subject?"

"Yes. I'll explain it to the doctor."

She said sternly, "Very well." Ten minutes later, the door by the receptionist opened, and an older nurse in a green uniform said, "Mr. Harris? Dr. Ishmael will see you now."

The nurse took him to an exam room. "Please remove your clothing except your undershorts and put on this gown." She pointed to a patterned gown on the table. "Put it on so the opening is in the back."

He followed her directions, and minutes later a boyish-looking doctor, perhaps early thirties, entered. "Mr. Harris? I'm Dr. Ishmael."

"Nice to meet you." They shook hands.

"What is it about your rectum?" asked the doctor. "Is it bleeding?"

"Yes."

"And how do you know? Have you noticed it in your stool?"

"Yes, when I wipe. And it hurts when I walk. I've felt it drip."

"I'm not going to futz with this. Let's send you to a specialist immediately, Dr. Kurtz. Fifth floor. I'll have Lucy draw up the proper forms, and you can go right down there." He picked up his phone and pushed his intercom button. "Lucy?"

Albert was having a hard time listening because his heart was pounding so loudly in his ears. A specialist?

Once he was dressed again on the fifth floor, Albert forgot the room number he was supposed to go to, even though the nurse had kept repeating it. He walked into the first office opposite the elevator, and he handed his papers to the woman in a nurse's uniform behind the desk. She stared at the papers as if they were moon rocks sent from Houston.

"Is this the place I'm supposed to be?" he asked.

"What doctor are you looking for?"

"I don't know. Dr. Lucy, maybe?"

"What're you going in for?"

"I'm... bleeding from my," he whispered and stopped. He let her eyes scan his papers further.

"Go to Room 516. Dr. Kurtz," she said with assurance.

He entered Room 516. The two women behind the desk smiled like the receptionist at his showroom. A big-ticket smile. "How may we help you?" said one of them. Albert handed his papers to her. "Who are you seeing?"

"Why does everyone ask that? Doesn't it say it there?"

"What're you coming in for?"

"To see the specialist, the... the..." He looked around. Waiting, there was only a Hispanic woman absorbed in a *Reader's Digest* and, very close to him, a silver-haired man in a wheel chair who didn't look as if he knew his name, let alone what a rectum was. "A rectal exam," said Albert in a whisper. "Or at least I assume that's what I'm here for."

"Yes," said the woman. "Rectal."

"What?" said the man in the wheel chair, rather loudly. "You need me now?"

"I didn't say Richard," emphasized the woman. "I said rectal. Just be calm, your ride will be here soon."

"Rectal?" said the man in the wheelchair to Albert. "My name's bad, too. Fishmeal. Richard Fishmeal." He turned to the woman again. "Shouldn't I be evacuated again?"

"Pay him no mind," the woman told Albert. "Please have a seat."

As Albert stepped to a seat, he noticed the woman with the *Reader's Digest* look at him funny. "Everyone's got one, Ma'am. Even you," said Albert, feeling as if he were being dissected.

It wasn't long before another nurse, one with glasses, called out Albert's name. She showed him to a room with a half-size metal table in it, the kind with butcher-block paper on a roll.

He imagined himself as fresh fish. She pulled on a fresh sheet of paper, then opened a cabinet where she found a paper gown. "Take off all your clothes and put this on, but don't tie it up in the back." She left and closed the door.

When Albert pulled down his underpants, he saw his makeshift napkin with a small wet spot of blood. He should show the doctor. A shelf under a cabinet was lined with urinary specimen jars, so Albert put his napkin in one of those.

Seconds after he finished with the gown, there was a knock on the door, and it opened before Albert said anything. A man in green surgical gear walked in with the same nurse who showed him the room. How did they know he was ready?

"Hi, I'm Dr. Kurtz. What seems to be the problem?"

Albert explained the bleeding, the difficulty walking, and the fact it still hadn't cleared up. He showed him the jar with his toilet paper. The doctor nodded with each bit of information.

"Please roll on your side facing the wall and curl up into a fetal position," Dr. Kurtz said while pulling on rubber gloves— yanking, stretching the gloves with a smile. The doctor opened a cabinet and pulled down something that looked like a microscope attached to a black bicycle pump. Albert maneuvered on the paper and mumbled that he felt like a ham hock.

"Pardon me?" said the doctor.

"Like this?" said Albert.

"Yes. That's a good position. This instrument, by the way, is called a sigmoidoscope. It's used to look at an S-shaped section of the colon between the descending section and the rectum in an area we call the sigmoid colon."

"A friend of mine had a colonoscopy once, and he had to clean out his colon first, drink a lot of—"

"I'm not going in that far. You don't have to be clean."

"Okay," Albert said warily.

"It's not going to feel very good, but it doesn't hurt, either. It's going to feel like you're going to have to evacuate, which is just fine, don't fight it."

The man dipped his finger into a Costco-sized jar of Vaseline and rubbed around Albert's anus. He pushed his finger in. Albert groaned, just as he had for his yearly prostate check-up. Why hadn't the doctors found anything at those times? They probably were in a hurry with a condo to buy or a nurse to hump.

The moment the sigmoidoscope pushed in, Albert felt strongly he had to move his bowels, and he grit his teeth, trying to stop it. No one told him he should have gone to the bathroom before this, and he imagined he must be making a mess. Albert saw reflected in the nurse's glasses how the doctor kept pushing the instrument while he kept his eye on the microscope end, twisting the flexible part this way and that. There is no death with dignity, thought Albert in the few brief moments where he relaxed his jaw. We all surrender our pride to doctors, and we slip away, one vital fluid at a time.

The doctor pulled out. "Done," he said. The nurse stood there, not having said a word. She nodded politely to Albert.

"What is it?" asked Albert to the doctor.

"You had an external thrombosis which has burst."

"Oh my God," Albert let out, imagining something akin to an appendix. When appendix burst, he knew, you die. He was getting light-headed fast. He felt as if he were falling, even though he was on the table.

"Don't misunderstand me," said the doctor. "It's another way to say you had a hemorrhoid, my friend. Because you waited so long, it's cured itself. Give yourself a sitzbath for the next few nights and call it a day."

"I don't have cancer or anything?"

"No, no. I looked all around. You're just fine. Nothing to worry about."

"Yes, yes, yes!" yelled Albert, and he was off the table, snapped his fingers like a leprechaun and gave a little dance. It lasted only a second until he realized he was fully exposed in the back.

"Nice to meet you, too," said the nurse with a laugh, and she and the doctor left.

* * *

Wade and Jazz parked in the parking structure next to the blue building owned by Cigna Healthcare. They took the stairs down the two flights, and Wade smelled urine in the air. Bums liked to pee in stairways. They walked apprehensively through the front door's unmarked and darkly tinted glass door.

Before Wade and Jazz could be tested, they each had to fill out a questionnaire, at the top of which were their code names. Jazz's was CL902. She assumed Wade's was CL901, as she insisted Wade take his form first.

They sat next to each other with their Number Two pencils and wrote. Her last test had been at the University of Southern California, the literary test that she had blown off. "Madame Bovary c'est moi," she had written at the end of her scathing essay, mimicking Flaubert, after she had cited specific teachers for destroying the beauty of fiction, calling them failed accountants. If this test was going to be like that one, she may as well do herself in now.

The first question was "Has your partner, or anyone who has had sex or used drugs with your partner, been found to have HIV infection or AIDS?"

Partner? That's an interesting word, thought Jazz. It's as full of hope as "love."

Wade and Jazz glanced at each other at the same moment. Wade touched her free hand lightly, like dusting sugar on strawberries. He returned to his page and circled the dot marked "Yes" to the first question.

"If 'Yes,' how long ago was the first such contact?" She glanced to his page and saw that he filled in the dot for "Less than three months." She penciled in the circle for "More than a Year." There was also a blank line in which they could write more specifically. She thought of writing about how she had been planning her and James's wedding when James told her his secret. She could have written that they had chosen the chicken dinner, not the rack of lamb, for their guests, and that her bridesmaids were to wear the color dusty rose. She wrote none of that.

The rest of the questionnaire addressed sexual practices, intravenous drug use, surgery, and blood transfusion. "Do you have sex when you are using drugs and alcohol?" Whoops. A big yes there.

She noticed her eyes were becoming watery as she wrote. Stop it, she told herself. And she finished the remaining questions quickly.

Wade saw the phlebotomist, the blood-drawing specialist, first. Wade returned a few minutes later and said, "Not bad. Like a mosquito bite."

"I hate mosquito bites," she said. He said nothing. "Even so, I'll go."

The phlebotomist, a man dressed in blue, reminded Jazz of Mr. Rogers—older, thin, with a smile that seemed pasted on. He effused a sense that he'd done this thousands of times. Good. After tying a thick, rubbery band around her upper arm, the man gently thumped one of Jazz's veins at the inside of her elbow with his forefinger. The vein rose immediately. The man inserted a needle, attached a small vial to the back of the needle, and then withdrew the band at the biceps. Blood flowed.

"Did it hurt?" Wade asked her when she came out. She felt dizzy. If she could only get to her seat. The phlebotomist dashed up behind her. "Here, have a cookie."

"Thanks," she said, not connecting that the cookie was something she should eat right then.

"It's okay. You're okay," Wade said and opened her cookie pack for her.

"We've got to wait two whole hours," she said with a cookie now in her mouth.

"Hey, it used to take days, I'm told."

"What're we going to do?"

"You need food, more than a cookie—some good ol' red meat. We can always go to Norm's for their cheapo steak-and-eggs."

"Can't we just stay here?"

"Sure."

They ate in the cafeteria. He had the hamburger plate; she had the veal patty.

Two hours later they returned for the results, squeezing each other's hands tightly as they checked in. A large, black nurse, as tall as Wade and probably a hundred pounds heavier, walked over and introduced herself as Violet. Her tag said Violet Jones, N.M.P.

"You two married?" Nurse Violet said to them.

"No," said Wade.

"Then I'll have to consult with you each individually unless you mutually consent otherwise. I want to remind you that these results are confidential and coded within our own records, so if you want to meet with me individually, that is perfectly acceptable."

That wasn't good news right there, thought Jazz. If it was good news, who would care about privacy?

"I'd just as soon Jazz was with me for my news," said Wade.

What the hell. "The same goes for me," said Jazz.

She directed them into a small room, not quite an office, as there were no pictures on the walls, not even a telephone on the plain wooden desk. They sat in plastic school chairs, and the nurse spoke to Wade first. "You wrote down that your last unprotected sexual contact was two weeks ago."

"Yes. With Jazz."

"I can tell you your test is negative, but two weeks is not long enough to be sure. The interval following infection and before the appearance of HIV antibodies is known as the serologic window period. After being infected with HIV, 95 percent of adults and youths will produce HIV antibodies within three months of infection—and 99 percent after six months. My suggestion is to come back in two and a half months for another test, to be sure."

"God. Really?" he blurted.

"Being negative after two weeks is a good sign, don't get me wrong," she said. "You just want to be sure."

"That's good," Jazz reassured Wade.

"Yes. Yes," he said, trying to believe it.

"And you," the nurse said, turning to Jazz. "I'm afraid yours came back positive. We're going to test your blood with a different test to be sure. That'll take a few more days."

Jazz could feel herself slide on the chair, and she compensated, pushed with her legs. She could feel Wade hold her arm, but that was no longer her arm. It was only on loan.

"I know you're not going to be open to a lot of information right now," said the nurse to Jazz, "but I'm here to answer any questions you have. I want to stress that you can remain healthy and productive for a long time—even a full, normal life—if you are positive. With the right attitude and the new drugs, you may not show any symptoms for many, many years."

"How many?" Jazz asked with the same kind of contempt she had shown a few of her English professors.

"I can't say. With the new innovations going on, maybe you won't ever get symptoms."

"But it's not like I am truly normal, right? I can't get married. I can't have kids."

"You can still get married. As for kids, you have options."

Options. Options are what you took on the stock market.

"There's a lot I can offer you," said Violet, "in terms of care and treatment. I'm available most days to discuss any questions that come up."

Out on the sidewalk, in the golden sun of late afternoon, Wade and Jazz stood apart under the falling petals of a purple jacaranda tree.

"I'm surprised you're still with me," Jazz said.

"What do you mean?"

"You're not my boyfriend."

"No, but I didn't want you to—"

"Thanks anyway. I can walk home from here." Jazz began to walk down the sidewalk away from Wade. He ran up to her.

"Let me take you home. What're you doing?"

"You've been nice, Wade, you really have. I couldn't have done this without you. Now I have to figure out my options."

"Let me help you," he said, pleading in his voice. "Like she said, it's all in attitude."

"And like I said, I'm sorry about what happened. I shouldn't have done it. You're a gorgeous guy, and I'm sure you can get another girlfriend tonight. Just don't ever have unprotected sex again."

"But I want you," he said, and he meant it.

"What do you mean you *want* me? You heard the news."

"So what?"

"I have the virus. Think about that. Even a condom is no absolute protection."

"I want to be with you."

"Oh, God," she said, shaking her head, looking at the ground, at all the fallen purple petals. "You don't know how this hurts me."

"*Why?*"

"I trusted James, and I've received the death penalty for it. Can you comprehend that? And then you call me up out of the blue, and you're so helpful, and I'm feeling like maybe life isn't so bad after all. In the end, though, I know it'll be me, alone."

"Not necessarily."

"Definitely," she said. "Don't you understand how everything works? In life, we rise until we reach a level of betrayal or disappointment. I've reached that. A crushed spirit won't let me go on."

"Listen," said Wade. "As crazy as this sounds. The last show I did, *Death of a Salesman*, I was trying to explain to the actress who played Linda, Willy's wife, about belief in a person. I think life is about seeing the greatness in a person, even when they're down. Right as I was telling her this, I knew I wanted to find such a person, someone I could believe in. I think that's partly why I was attracted to you that night. I'd heard you talking to your girlfriend. You were saying she had to finish her degree, had to get her own credit line, be her own person as you were going to do. That impressed me."

Jazz was looking up now. She opened her mouth, but at first nothing came out. "I know this may sound stupid," she said, "but—"

"No, no," he said. "I don't want to hear anything else."

"One question," she said. "Don't you feel cheated some-how—that life was supposed to be good, and then you got bad luck?"

"I don't believe in luck, good or bad. I believe in probability."

"Was it probable that we'd meet?"

"No, but you meet new people each week. It's probable one of those people, if not many, would find you incredible. I find you incredible, and—"

"But I may have given you—"

"That's not bad luck. It's just numbers again. I'm not going to blame—"

"But—"

"Shh." He put his arm around her, and she did not pull away. "Use what's given you to best advantage, I say." With the barest touch of his finger, his guidance, she moved her face upwards. He kissed her.

* * *

The oddest thing. Albert sat in the examination room, and he didn't know what to do next. He hadn't planned on being alive. He felt good, he did. But it made him wonder what he should do. These were extra moments, abundant moments, and how should he celebrate? He dialed Brenda from his cell phone. He had to tell Brenda. He'd been holding too much back.

No one answered. She was probably shopping. The more he thought about it, she'd probably make a joke about his hemorrhoid, saying it probably had more hair than his face. He hung up. He had to do something good, think this all through. Maybe he'd go to Norm's, treat himself to the Steak and Eggs breakfast that was good all day. There's a treat.

He looked at the people carefully as he walked toward the waiting room, to the nurse and to Dr. Kurtz who nodded to him, to a short man carrying towels, with his name, Salim, stitched on his blue shirt, to the red-uniformed young man vacuuming. Everyone had their own place while they were alive, didn't they? People were just random protoplasm that somehow fell into an order. It may not be grand, but it meant something. The whole office here, for instance, required a number of people who, with their chaotic lives, came together and allowed for Albert to be looked at so carefully. It made him smile.

When he opened the door to the waiting room, not only was Richard Fishmeal still there, but so were Brenda and Timothy, both looking concerned.

"And?" said Brenda instantly.

"How?" he said, trying to comprehend how this was possible, astounded, even utterly pleased they were there. The universe was an amazing place. "How'd you know I was here?"

"Stan," Brenda said. "He said you had to go to the doctor. You didn't tell me, so that kind of explained a lot. I called your physician who told me you're here, with Kurtz, a proctologist. That sounded worrisome, so we came. Are you all right?"

"Yeah, Dad, are you?" said Timothy. "Sorry about the bald jokes this morning."

"I'm fine. Hey, family," Albert said, catching both of them by their necks with his elbows and pulling them in. "You fuckin' drive me crazy."

"Fucking about time," said Timothy.

* * *

Wade suggested they rent bicycles at the Santa Monica pier and just try to take the day a moment at a time. He told her whenever he felt confused, bicycling helped clear him up.

"Yes—I'd love to," she heard herself say and meant it. She was feeling rather lightheaded after the kiss, and the feeling had not stopped. Only holding onto his hand steadied her. Whatever this guy was made out of, she wanted it. She would figure out her life and options tomorrow. Today, she thought, would be today.

They walked to the parking structure, and to avoid the smell in the stairwell, they took the elevator. By inspiration, she pushed the button for the roof. Perhaps they could see the beach from there, she said, and then they could just walk down to the car. He nodded with a grin. Everything was okay with him.

Up on the roof, with the wind in their hair, they could not see the beach, but the moment was somehow perfect, as if she could fly. They were taller than the feather-duster palm trees, their tall reedy trunks gently bending in the wind. A pelican seemed frozen in the air, riding a minor jet stream above them. Whatever he was thinking, he seemed happy because he gave her a smile. She looked toward the sun, feeling its warmth on her skin. Wade seemed to notice.

"The sun is almost all hydrogen," he said. "That's all it burns."

"When's it going to run out?"

"It has enough to last, oh, another 4.5 billion years."

"A little longer than us."

"Yeah."

"We're bigger than dinosaurs," she said.

He looked as if he were going to ask her what that meant when she said, "Do you remember the Flintstones?"

"The cartoon, you mean?"

"Yeah. I liked the theme song. When I was a kid, everything was so simple."

He started to sing it. "Flintstones, Meet the Flintstones. They're the modern stone age family..."

Jazz heard another music intrude. She turned her head and saw a Volvo swing around the corner, heading toward them for the exit ramp. The music was the Hallelujah chorus from Handel's *Messiah*. "Hallelujah! Hallelujah!" the occupants boomed, while Wade, having skipped a few lines, was already singing, "When you're with the Flintstones...!"

The Volvo accelerated. The car's "Hallelujahs" rose. Wade, like a bird, like a misguided falcon not sensing danger in his flight path, let go of Jazz's hand and broke into a tap dance as if to really do the silly song justice. With a few simple steps—so simple, she didn't even anticipate them—his dance took him right into the line of the car as he bellowed, "Yabba Dabba Do Time!"

"Wade!" Jazz yelled.

Wade's legs kissed the chrome bumper, which tipped him backward, and the Volvo's grill slammed into his buttocks. Wade flew. Jazz saw him soar, and time slowed. She screamed. His arms twirled and for a second it looked like he might stay in the air. If only, if only.

* * *

Albert had seen the young man too late. Brenda and Timothy shouted something guttural as Albert's foot crushed the brakes. The car screeched to a stop.

Albert undid his seatbelt and shoved open the door. The young man was crumpled on the ground, not moving, and a young woman—she must have been walking with the young man—screamed and ran to him. Was he dead? How could this happen? Why would the man run in front of his car?

As Albert stood, the young man pushed himself off of the ground, turning his head left and right. He was alive! The young woman knelt down. "Stay down, stay down. You might have hurt your neck or something."

"Wow," said the young man, sitting, confused looking, brushing himself off. "That was something."

Albert stepped forward, light-headed, seeing checkerboards, struggling to walk. "Are— Are—" was all he could get out. He couldn't add, "you okay?" because he thought he was going to faint.

Albert had to sit, wondering if he were having a heart attack. His breath just wasn't coming. Wasn't there supposed to be a pain in the arm? Heart attacks were supposed to be painful. Why couldn't he breathe? He couldn't die today. Albert saw the young man at his level staring at him, worried.

"Dad!" Timothy said, freeing himself from the car. "Are you okay?" Soon Albert heard Brenda's footsteps, too, rushing toward him.

Albert realized life had too much damn irony. If he could just breathe and if that young man could be okay, he'd appreciate things more. Please, God. Please, whomever. What do I have to do?

Albert simply took a deep breath, and doing so started to clear his head. Concentrate. Take another breath. While he could feel his heart beating hard, he now breathed more easily.

Albert started to stand.

"Stay down, Dad!"

"No, I'm all right. Must have been information overload." Timothy and Brenda were at each of Albert's arms, helping him up, and the sun felt good on his face and head. The breeze smelled sweet, not of salt but of newly mown grass—odd for being so close to the beach.

The young man stood, too, aided by the woman. "I'm sorry," said the young man to the woman. "I'm sorry," he repeated, looking at Albert.

"I'm sorry, too," said Albert. "My God, it happened so fast. What's going on?"

"I don't know," said the young man. "I didn't mean to scare you."

"Anything broken?" said the young woman. "Check your legs, your butt," and her hands glided over him as if reading Braille.

"I'm fine," said the young man.

"Let's take him to the hospital," said Brenda.

"Do you know how you scared me—scared us!" said the young woman, who now held the young man in splendor as if meeting him after a long absence at an airport.

"I feel lucky," said the young man.

"Luck had nothing to do with it," said the young woman.

"I don't know," said Brenda. "Something is miraculous here."

"Fuck—it's statistics," added Timothy, who joined with his mother to give Albert a group hug.

Albert closed his eyes, relishing every second. Whatever caused this concurrence of events—caused him to meet his wife, caused him to have his son, on and on—he didn't care. He was thankful. When he pulled away, he extended his hand to the young woman. "I'm Albert."

"Jazz," she said, offering her own, grinning, happy. Everyone introduced each other, there beneath the brontosaurus sun.

A
Shoe
Falls

M ax was awakened when a shoe, a white low-heeled one from above, hit him in the head. He bolted upright in bed like a six-foot mousetrap sprung into action, and he gasped for breath. Once recovered, he tried to comprehend where he was.

As Max now focused on the room—on the many dressers and piles of magazines and boxes and clothes arranged in stacks—he thought he might be in a warehouse. The black cat staring at him from the dresser next to the bed reminded him he was in his otherwise white bedroom.

He'd been dreaming. He'd been in a crowded cab. The cab had taken him around the San Fernando Valley all night with the Marx Brothers—Groucho, Chico, Harpo, and Zeppo. He smiled, recalling that before he had fallen asleep, he had been watching the Marx Brothers' *A Night at the Opera* on AMC. In his dream, squished with all the brothers in the back seat, he tried to explain that he was perfectly sane, "Really, no truly," but the Marx Brothers weren't buying it, and they wanted a fish to be a flashlight. The cab driver drove for hours around Los Angeles' crowded freeways, passing again and again a restaurant, Roscoe's Chicken and Waffles. The cab's meter had just passed beyond $150,000. Thanks to the cat, Max had been driven from the cab into reality by a shoe to the head.

Max smiled as he grasped that he didn't owe any money at all to the cab driver. There was no cab driver. He had saved thousands of dollars by waking up.

His sudden charge into the real world must have awakened his wife, Alice, who, a foot shorter, was turning over as he looked at her. "What time is it?" she asked.

He glanced at his clock-radio. "Almost six."

"Why'd you wake me?"

"I didn't. The cat shoved a shoe on me, and I jerked up."

"Good girl," she said with a laugh and rolled back over.

Max frowned at yet another disrespectful comment of hers. He thought about the true meaning of the dream, and he asked himself: if the ride was getting so expensive and monotonous, why hadn't he asked the cab driver to let him off? Why hadn't he done more than sit there, bouncing in the back seat pondering his sanity? He was a passive man, goddamn it.

"Are you getting up to correct papers or what?" Alice said with her eyes closed.

"Yeah. I'm getting up."

"You assign too much writing."

Max looked at the cat with fleas, the shoes, the room, the blanket's foothills, and his wife underneath. "This is no way to live," he mumbled.

"What?" said Alice.

He said more loudly, "How will my students learn writing if they don't write?" He then realized: how would he live if he didn't live? Stop being passive. He had to do something for himself. He had been married almost twelve years, and that was enough. He was almost forty. Today was the day he was going to change things. He would leave.

With that, he lifted the covers, moved to the edge, and stood decisively. As he buttoned a fresh, starched shirt, he thought about how he would announce his departure. Maybe he should call it a trial separation—it's easier that way.

"What?" Alice might say. "You met another woman?"

"No, it was thanks to a dream," he would say. He would pause.

"So you did meet another woman," she'd say.

"No, it was a dream—which isn't as nice as meeting another woman, though clearer."

"So you met another woman?"

"No, but I've kept hoping I might." He wouldn't say that, though it was true. He kept hoping he might meet a woman— someone to have just a quickie affair with. Perhaps he'd meet a voluptuous, newly single mother of one of his fifth-grade students, or maybe he would approach the new kindergarten teacher, Danielle. She was barely out of grad school, only twenty-six years old, thin, with a penchant for wearing dresses that made her even more feminine, like Audrey Hepburn in her early films. Max sometimes caught himself staring at Danielle walking across the schoolyard with her class in a neat line behind her like little ducks, her long light brown hair, curled like fingers seeking skin, bouncing on her back.

Dawn was breaking as Max yanked on his gray pressed pants. He could see more details of the bedroom in the growing light. Alice loved shoes. Flats, low heels, medium heels, high heels. Brown ones, red ones, gold ones—a whole Dr. Seuss universe of shoes. They encircled their bed. The dressers were sprinkled with his wife's shoes, like Indians on mesas. Shoes lined the floor of not just their mutual walk-in closet, but in the spare bedroom closet, too. Alice recently had started buying cardboard boxes with cubbyhole inserts. Each cubbyhole held a pair of shoes. Three such boxes now stood on top of each other, filled with shoes, blocking most of one French door. It was now hard to see out.

As Max brushed his teeth in his bathroom, he imagined that his lawyer, the one he did not have yet, would look at him and ask, "You're leaving her because she has too many shoes?"

"I'm a foreigner in my own house," he'd have to explain.

"It's another woman," his lawyer would say.

"No. I couldn't attract another woman if I were honey and she were a fly."

Max was troubled about leaving Neddy, though. He was only seven, slender as new bamboo. Still, better to do this while he's younger—and better first talk with Alice alone, without Neddy nearby. In an hour, when he had to wake them up to start the day, he'd throw Neddy in the shower, along with Neddy's waterproof list of spelling words. Max had already prepared the special slate for Neddy for his test today, including the words "harmony," "sincerity," and "potato." Alice would drag herself out of bed and prepare her tea. He'd tell her then, in the perpetually messy-from-her kitchen.

As Max returned to his bedroom for socks, he noticed another cat, Princess, her butt poised over his new clock radio.

"Oh my god, no!" Max whispered loudly so he wouldn't wake Alice, who was back asleep. Princess let a stream of urine escape, and it bubbled right into the holes for the speaker. As Max grabbed her, she stopped peeing, but still he wanted to scream. He couldn't if he didn't want to wake Alice. He wasn't ready to confront his wife again.

He threw Princess out the back door. The damn cat kept peeing on anything electronic, but it was Alice's favorite cat. She wouldn't scold it. Princess torpedoed his laptop computer one evening, and he had to pay $200 in servicing, as pee wasn't covered under warranty. Also hit was his synthesizer keyboard, a present to himself and on which he had mastered "Down in the Valley" before the thing shorted out. Now his clock radio. His all-news station would probably sound as if it were coming from underwater, if it worked at all. In the past, the angrier he had become with Princess, the more Alice seemed to adore the cat. Fine. He would not argue. Maybe he should teach it to pee on shoes before he moved out.

Max's office was in the basement in a nook next to the water heater and the furnace. Max sat at his desk. He'd always meant to fix up his office, get a real desk instead of a door on top of two cheap filing cabinets, but what he had was clean and efficient. He turned on his computer. He realized he needed to compose a speech to Alice. If he was going to follow through on leaving her, then he needed a clear explanation of why. The best way to be clear was to write down a first draft as fast as possible, without worry about grammar. The best writing, as he told his fifth graders, comes from polishing. Rewrite and re-write. This will lead you to clarity. As for giving speeches, Max told them to be animated and be focused. He had to make his announcement to Alice animated and focused.

"Alice," he would say, "you know and I know we're more like roommates than lovers."

"Roommates more than lovers? What's this lover shit?" she'd probably say in response. "Lovers are something you have in an affair. Are you having an affair?"

Max erased *lovers* and replaced it with *a married couple,* and he continued typing. "The point is, I'm just kind of like wallpaper here anyway." What kind? With stripes or flowers? Self-adhesive? He erased the sentence and wrote a new one: "I'm like the Maytag repairman."

"What the hell're you talking about?" she'd probably say.

"I'm not vital, but kind of useful, like a repairman is useful. I'm the guy who pays the bills, mows the lawn, and runs out to the store when you need an onion. Otherwise, you don't really want me around much."

The hot-water heater's gas flame burst on, a mini-explosion, making Max jump. He had never gotten used to the way the gas heater popped into action right next to his desk. The gas people said the heater was normal, safe. He pictured a possible headline: "Burned and Scalded Body of Teacher Found in Basement." He had wanted the spare bedroom for his office, but Alice insisted it be her sewing room. She hadn't sewn a god-damn thing in years.

"I'm lower on the scale than your sewing machine," he wrote. "I'm lower on the scale than the spiders crawling around my desk in the basement."

"It's your fucking basement," she'd say.

It was true. Los Angeles didn't have many basements, but he had loved them in Iowa, where he'd grown up, so when he and Alice shopped for a house, he insisted on a basement. They found such a house in Culver City. Their front yard had a single Jacaranda tree that blossomed into a breathtaking purple each spring. The tree sold her on the house, while the basement was the winning point for him.

"The point is," he wrote, "I'm no longer important to you. We don't converse, we bicker. We don't talk about interesting things, we complain." He wrote "we complain," even though it was "you complain."

"I'm keeping Neddy," she would say soon enough, not even trying to talk him out of leaving, he foresaw. He couldn't expect differently. She was intelligent and capable enough, and the court would side with her. So be it. He couldn't change cultural history. Neddy would cry. Seven-year-olds don't take such news well. Max had been seven when his dad had left. He had cried.

"I've found an apartment near here," Max wrote, needing to end his speech. "I've put down first and last month's rent, and I'll get the movers to come on Saturday for my stuff."

"What stuff?" she would say, ready to claim almost everything, ready to fight.

"My clothes and office," he would say. "We can discuss the rest with our lawyers." His apartment was as imaginary as his lawyer, but he could get both in an afternoon. Now just to do the deed.

As he walked up the stairs, Max sensed his heart beating hard, and his feet felt particularly heavy. He was getting light-headed. What if he fell down the stairs and broke his neck? She'd probably get the insurance money and remember him as a saint.

Max opened the door at the top. He could already hear Neddy's voice. "But I like bacon!" Neddy said.

"Last night you didn't eat your chicken because you said you wanted to be a vegetarian," said Alice. "You said you didn't like animals being killed."

"Yeah, but bacon's okay," explained Neddy. "Who cares about pigs?"

Max could hear Alice burst out in laughter. She did have a sweet laugh. "You can't be a part-time vegetarian," said Alice.

"Then can't you just make chicken better?" asked Neddy.

Alice groaned. "I should be insulted," she said. "But I'll make you bacon anyway."

"Thanks, Mommy."

It was unusual for Alice and Neddy to be up so soon. Max was unprepared to meet them this second. His heart beat faster. He began to think: what if it beat faster and faster until, well, until he plopped over dead there in the hallway, which was lined with all his photographs. His head would probably smash against one glass frame on his way down. "Teacher Found Underneath Shards of Glass."

"Is that you, Daddy?" Neddy said and popped into the hallway. Neddy ran with his feet skitch skitch skitching in the hallway, and he wrapped his arms around Max's legs.

Alice peered around the corner. Her face instantly showed concern. "You okay, honey?"

"I'm, ah... I was just..." His breath was coming short. What the hell was his body doing to him? Max now sensed every little thing: the way the light cast his long shadow on the white wall, the way his stammering voice reverberated, the way the air smelled of bacon. Neddy looked up proudly at him. Alice frowned even more and stepped into the hallway, concerned. The two cats froze in their tracks as if Max were a tree branch about to fall. He leaned against the wall. "I was just exercising," he blurted out. "Still need to catch my breath."

"Really? You're okay?"

"Yeah," said Max.

"Could you finish cooking Neddy's bacon?" she asked as she walked toward him. She was wearing the green silk pajamas he'd bought her. Her nipples suggested themselves and, like two synchronized skaters on verdigris ice, moved in an intricate pattern across the front as she approached. She had beautiful breasts. That's not what he should be thinking, he reminded himself. It's time he cast the first stone.

"I've been thinking and— Neddy, you hop in the shower right now, okay?" he asked.

"You're supposed to make me more bacon," Neddy protested.

"He can't take a shower, I have to," Alice interjected. "If you wanted him to shower, you should have come up earlier."

Max looked at his watch. It was already seven thirty. How could that be? He never worked past seven in his office. "Why didn't you yell down to me?" he asked Alice.

"I started coming down," she said, "but I heard you grunting and typing so fervently, I didn't want to disturb you."

"I wasn't grunting."

"Then what does *uh-uh-uh-uh* sound like to you? Grunting. Did whatever you write come out well?"

"We have to talk," Max heard himself say.

"Can't. You finish Ned's bacon, and I'll shower," said Alice. With a wink, she pecked his lips with hers and was off. Things just weren't going well.

Neddy pulled on his arm toward the kitchen, while Alice, pushing into the bedroom, choked on the smell. "Phew! A cat peed in here somewhere."

Max followed her into the bedroom. "Princess. Right into my new clock radio."

"You just have to get rid of that cat," said Alice.

"You like that cat," Max said to Alice.

"I don't. You keep saying I do. She's your cat." And Alice stepped closer to the bathroom.

Max didn't want it over yet. In a moment Alice would be out of his reach. The door was closing. He had to say something. "What about all these... these damn shoes!"

"Daddy said a swear word, Daddy said a swear word," chirped Neddy, who had followed behind.

"I'm sorry," he said to Neddy. "Don't do as I do."

"Yes, I have too many shoes," Alice agreed. "I told you I'm cleaning them out. Most of them are going."

"And this place is such a *mess!*" Max added.

"It'll all be cleaned up once I get this stuff to Goodwill."

"And what about all these phone messages from 10 B.C.," he said pointing to old notes under her shoes.

Alice stepped closer. "What's wrong with you this morning?" she said. "Did I do something wrong? You've been patient with me and my shoes, but today you're an absolute bear."

"Oh, that's positive reinforcement," Max said.

"I can't win, can I? Whatever I did, I'm sorry."

"But, but—"

She kissed his cheek and moved off into the bathroom. He was frozen, as if in the beam of someone's headlights.

"Daddy! Bacon's burning!"

Cripes. Neddy was right. The smell was there, though the smoke wasn't yet. He dashed into the kitchen, saw the fork next to the pan, and quickly flipped the bacon over. "Burned, like my life," he mumbled to himself.

"I like mine crisp," said Neddy.

Max laid the bacon out on the waiting paper towels.

"Daddy, I don't like so much grease. Can't you press them like Mommy does?"

Everyone's a critic, Max thought as he patted the bacon with another paper towel. He gave a strip to Neddy and then noticed a spot, a stain, on his shoe. Bacon grease. Taking another paper towel, he wiped the spot. It didn't go away. The spot was merely shinier.

Max knew in that instant that he wasn't going to do anything about Alice. He would continue on while his heart beat. His life was just one big cab ride into the sky.

Neddy ate his bacon with a crunch and a smile. He pushed a strip into his mouth as if it were on a conveyor belt, and his teeth had become a cutter bar. Neddy laughed, as if that was how simple the world was. Life was much more complicated, though, thought Max—as complex as a fish becoming a flashlight. Neddy just didn't know.

The Holes In My Door

S ometime past three in the afternoon, as I slugged back my fourth gelatinous protein shake of the day—the stuff was supposed to increase my muscle mass but all I felt from it was woozy—I heard three distinct shots. Bam, bam, bam, bam! Make that four.

The sounds made me spit up a mouthful of the tan cocktail into the plastic container from which I drank. "Did you hear that?" I yelled, without thinking, still used to assuming Bonita was there. My wife had left me over a year before, sick and tired of what she called my fixations. At the time I was going through a period of abstinence. (Not impotence, as she could plainly feel some nights, her roving hands nearly ruining it for me.) It was only month two. Just a month to go. I'd simply read that if a man kept his sperm to himself, he'd be more vital and aware. There was even evidence his IQ would rise an average of ten points. I could use all the IQ I could get. It's a dog-eat-dog world out there. It didn't mean I didn't love Bonita—but Bonita fled.

With the shots still ringing in my ears, fear now overwhelmed me. Who was shooting out in the alley? I grabbed the phone, shaking, and dialed 911. "Nine-one-one emergency," came an efficient female voice, not unlike that of Bonita.

"I heard shots just now—in the alley," I blurted.

"Your name?"

"Frank Spielberg." My last name was Philo, but I inserted an impressive last name. Maybe she'd think I was Steven's brother, be more efficient, and consider my life important.

"Are you sure they were shots?" she asked.

"There were four quick ones in a row—you don't get that with a car backfiring." Backfiring was what Bonita and I had always called such noises, not wanting to admit they might be something else. But not this time.

"What are the nearest cross streets to the alley?"

"Pleasantview and Line. Line Street and Pleasantview."

"I show an alley runs south and north near there. Did the shots come from the south of that intersection, or north?"

"I don't know! It was somewhere near there!"

"We'll send a cruiser by."

I thanked her and hung up. A cruiser, she said? Cruising is what you do as a teenager when you want to pick up chicks or eat a couple of Big Macs.

As I waited, an overwhelming sense of doom choked me. It was as if the person who'd fired the gun was blessed with ultrasensitive hearing like a Spandexed superhero gone awry. He knew I'd called the police and needed to kill me. It was an irrational thought, but at the time it kept pounding at me like the commercials on TV for Whoppers. I had to leave the house.

As I ran out the door into the afternoon sun and toward the garage, I briefly considered whether I should first call Jungle Woman, the "movie-loving late-twenties restaurant manager" whom I'd met online with my computer on something called Single Catches. Jungle Woman and I would type for hours to each other, express our innermost feelings about lost love and such topics as the late actor Peter Lorre and meat loaf (the food, not the musician). She had finally offered me her phone number and her real name: Pam. I'd discovered her wonderful, caring voice, and that she adored Hitchcock films as much as I did. We'd talked a long time, and when I said "LMIRL", she knew the cyber lingo for "let's meet in real life," and she said "absolutely yes."

On my way to our first meeting at a donut shop near me, I'd wondered what if she were a club-footed hunchback? What if she had breath like a fire hose of methane? I'd found instead a beautifully smiling woman slightly rotund but with lovely long dark hair thick as a rain forest. She liked my boyish, honest face, she said. I, too, was rotund, thanks to my weight gain after Bonita had left. We were bees to honey. This very night we were to meet at the Nuart Cinema—our mutual passion for film. I couldn't call her now. I had to run like a refugee.

I was so preoccupied with leaving that only after I opened the garage door to the alley and jammed the white Volvo sedan into reverse did I see that the back window was completely shattered. Other than a single oval hole, the glass was so crinkled I could not see through it. The front windshield, too, was just as crenulated. I yelled and jumped out as if the car glowed at a thousand degrees.

Two children, around eleven, dressed for baseball, saw me leap out as they walked down the alley, and they gave me a look as if I were insane—the same kind of look I'd given to Mr. Reilly when I was a kid. My cousins and I dubbed Mr. Reilly the "Madman of Maplewoods" after we had witnessed the gaunt man try to shoot chipmunks with his .22 rifle. You had to be demented to consider the cute creatures pests.

I leaped at the garage wall and pressed the button that made the wooden garage door go down. After it thumped close, I was bathed in near darkness and perceived four beams of sunlight from four holes in the garage door. Motes danced in the light's streams. I clicked on the garage light. The door and the back of my car needed examination, even if I was still shaking.

In addition to the broken window, my Swedish chariot had one hole through a brake light and a big dime-sized hole in the trunk. A line of steel gleamed on the top of the trunk as if the bullet had been Moses parting the sea of paint. The bullet must have skidded along the top until it hit the lip of steel that held the bottom of the back window. That lip must have forced the bullet up. Sure enough, I could see a bit of silver winking at me from a wooden beam in the ceiling. The fourth hole in the garage door matched the height of the rear window.

I clicked open the garage door to run. The cruiser—a standard black-and-white with disco lights—almost hit me as it slammed on its brakes.

"What the hell—" said the Hispanic officer in his dark blue uniform.

"I've been shot!" I screamed.

The man and his husky white partner jumped out. "Where?" said the first cop.

"In the rear!"

The white cop, who had a pockmarked face and a chin like the crack on the Liberty Bell, dashed over and joined the driver in bending to peer at my buttocks.

"Not me!" I said. "My CAR!" And I pointed.

"Oh, *yeah*," said the Hispanic officer. His name, Jones, I caught on his badge, which caught me off guard. The other cop's badge proclaimed him as Bleak. Why not go all the way and change it to Grim Reaper?

Jones scrutinized the car as I had. Bleak went back to the cruiser and pulled out a clipboard and a form. He asked me basic questions such as my name and address. Meanwhile Jones bounced into the front seat and after a few minutes he shouted, "I found it!"

"Found what?" I asked, running away from Bleak.

"A slug," he uttered with pride. "Your front windshield doesn't have a hole, see? The bullet had to go somewhere." He scooped it out of the rubber seal near the bottom of the window. He used the thin blade of a Swiss Army knife, which still had its ivory-colored toothpick.

He weighed the slug in his hand. "Twenty-five caliber," he said assuredly. "These come from one of those cheap pistols, a Saturday Night special. Probably some young kid trying out his new gun."

In this society I was now a rifle range? "What do I do?" I asked seriously.

"Move," laughed Bleak.

Jones glanced to a boy, about twelve years old, thin and delicate, who rode his small bicycle past us like a butterfly on rubber wheels. The kid scowled at the police. "There's a little gang member right there," said the cop.

"He's in a gang?" At that age I was home watching *The Wonder Years* and *Growing Pains*."

"He may be the kid who did it," Bleak said. "In the old days, we might stop and search him. Or we might go to the Taco Bell down the street and search everyone there. We can't do those things now, so we just fill out reports after the fact."

"You'd search a whole restaurant?"

He tore off a duplicate of the form he'd been working on from his clipboard. He handed the yellow sheet to me. "This long number here, that's what you'll be giving to your insurance company. You have insurance, don't you?"

I nodded. I could picture the file in my mind. The file would be in the red section marked "Bills," in the green Pendaflex marked "Insurance," in the manila folder labeled "House." After Bonita left, I had decided to organize my home office better—spent three non-stop days at it. I was getting my life in order, even if some nights I could only stare at the cracks on the ceiling.

The police drove off, and I gazed at my dead car. What was left should just run me over. Or maybe I should put my lips around the tail pipe. No. I had to move forward as Pam, Jungle Woman, once typed. I couldn't see her that evening, though— too many things to do. I left her a message that I was canceling but gave no explanation. Next I spackled the holes in the door and then painted them to show the hoodlum who had done this that I did not rest. A call to the insurance company brought a mobile auto glass unit that replaced the two windows and gave me an appointment for bodywork. And then I washed my hands a lot, at least once an hour for the next two days. I couldn't help myself—they itched otherwise. The compulsion stopped, to my relief, after I had an idea of what to do next. I hurried down to Gun Heaven on Olympic Boulevard. I needed protection.

Though I had for years been anti-gun, it was clear that society would rather shoot it out with me. After all, every other movie poster showed some handsome Wesley Snipes type or lissome Rachel Weiss-like waif with a big fat gun. Guns were sexy. Guns were effective. Why fight it?

Gun Heaven lay like a shark-toothed guppy in a pod mall near a hospital and next to a Pioneer Chicken restaurant. I imagined someone munching on a drumstick, then waddling over to Gun Heaven with greasy fingers, wanting to pull a trigger or two.

I walked into Gun Heaven, which seemed as bright as a toy store. A large man, slightly balding, said, "Can I hep ya?" He sounded Southern.

"I need protection," I said.

"You've come to the right place."

He started with a brown-handled handgun that he withdrew from under the glass counter. "Now, whatcha got here, let's call it the starting point, is the Nef Lady Ultra at 32 caliber," said Hartmut—that was his name on his tag—holding out a handgun with a four-inch barrel. "Blue finish as you see, walnut-finished hardwood, with a weight of only 31 ounces. I start here because it's only 149 dollars. If you want something a little more substantial," he said, alluding to my manhood perhaps, "This here's the EAA Windicator."

He showed me a model with a six-inch barrel. "A 357 magnum, it has a six load capacity and, believe me, with one of the new Remington Golden Saber hollow-point loads, you can put a hole the size of a quarter into anything you want."

Hartmut apparently had not shaved in three days and his eyes, his whole face, was quite red. His skin, especially below his eyes, hung like the face of a basset hound. He must have been a drinker, though he seemed plenty sober to me. Behind him, in lighted glass case after case, stood so many guns, an army could be outfitted. I didn't touch either gun, overwhelmed by it all.

"Now I know what you're going through, a sense of violation, a need to stand up to any possible intruder," Hartmut continued without any prompting.

"People don't have any morals or manners anymore," I said, feeling his openness to understand. "A couple weeks ago I was watering my front lawn when I saw three teenagers pushing each other in front of the barbershop. One kid pushed too hard, and his friend fell against the huge plate glass window at the barbershop. It shattered. Know what they did? Just laughed and walked away. And neither me or the barber ran after them or said anything because, who knows, maybe these kids had a gun."

"And all these carjackings going on," Hartmut added. "Why succumb when you could sneak your own gun up and blast them off the road!"

"You can have a gun in the car?" I asked innocently.

He straightened up his back and glanced at the young man in a suit behind the counter who must have been his boss. "No," said Hartmut formally. "You can't conceal a weapon without a permit, and the city gives permits to no one." Then he leaned in conspiratorially. "But bad guys don't carry permits. You think the kid who hit your garage had one? You think the druggies with Chinese SKS semi-autos turned into automatics and fifty-round magazines have one?"

"I just want something for the house," I said. "Isn't a rifle better?"

Hartmut grinned as if I had given him a hundred birthday roses. "My friend. The best thing you could get is a shotgun. He waved me over to a case down the way and pulled out a double-barreled gun which he called a Merkel 20-gauge Model 47E. "This is the best value for the money, made in East Germany—well, it's not East Germany anymore, but you know what I mean. What I'd do is saw the barrels down to 44 inches, which is still legal, but it'll give you a nice, wide spread. You'll hit whoever's after you."

"Won't that damage the house?" I asked, imagining my walls as thin and deteriorated as the Taco Bell wrappers in the street.

Hartmut looked at me as if I'd just fallen off the proverbial turnip truck. "Are you worried about a few scratches on your house or your life?"

"How many guns do you own yourself, Hartmut?"

"Two hundred fifty three, including the T-2i Lasersight I just bought."

The answer somehow endeared him to me. And it's not that Hartmut was the Music Man of gun sales—and nothing rhymed with G and stood for gun right there in River City—but Hartmut sold me. I not only bought the shotgun and a dozen packs of shells, but I also signed up for a year's subscription to *Guns and Ammo* magazine before I left. (I had a lot of ammunition, but as Hartmut said, "Never know if there'll be another riot.")

I put the black-barreled gun, unsawed, under my bed for a few days. I could feel its power when I went to bed each night. I wanted to call Pam about this, but this wasn't a time to become involved. And strangely, I heard noises outside each night, things I had never noticed from my room before—an odd, loud cawing, for instance. Couldn't be a bird—few birds are active at night. Must be a robber calling to his cohort, like the bandits did in Westerns as they surrounded unsuspecting pioneers. Another time I heard a glass bottle drop out in the alley, but it didn't break. That could be someone climbing up over the garbage cans and the wall.

At each odd noise, I'd reach under my bed and bring out the shotgun. The assailants, too, must have felt its power as no one bothered me, much as I dared them to in my mind.

My gun. The protector. After owning it a week, I asked myself if I *really* knew how to use it. Was I just going to assume I could shoot it when the time came? How much kick did it have—would it surprise me? What kind of spread did it give?

And could I assume it would be reliable? After all, it had never been shot. It was a virgin, as I was in a sense. But where would I try it? Someone's garage door? No, I could visit the desert, out near Lancaster.

Once, when Bonita and I had loved each other, when we lived together and groped for each other and performed sex acts as in the movies (well, in the movies I now sometimes rent), we had heard about land in Lancaster from a short door-to-door salesman, a man named Fred with hair bright and gray as a cat. Fred was friendly. He told us how he'd arrived from Cairo twenty years before, penniless but educated. He'd eked out a living teaching math, but then he realized in America you needed to own things, particularly land. He started small, as he suggested we do. "Now I have a huge home in Beverly Hills. Beverly Hills," he said again, pronouncing it enthusiastically as if it were whipped butter icing on a glorious wedding cake. His gold chains on his wrists danced.

Fred spoke about our owning two acres that he had—acres!—out in Lancaster, where we'd never been before. At the time, Bonita and I were renting a cute, shack-like house with window boxes on a postage stamp-sized lot. He pulled out an official map of Lancaster, which showed a new, proposed airport a few miles away from the land. It would only be a matter of years before the area would be like the rest of L.A., houses crowded together like tea cups on a glass shelf. Ten thousand dollars for two such acres was cheap.

After several of his visits, we bought his land. Fred took our check and gave us the deed and a map to it with a big grandfatherly hug. Months later, we visited our two acres—and were crushed. We felt conned. Sure, we had two acres, but two acres in vast nothingness: tumbleweeds, a dirt road, and a line of telephone poles. It was like owning a crater on the moon—what good would it do? Now it could do me some good. I would go try my shotgun there.

I had not been back to the land for ten years, but found the original map from Fred in my files under the yellow "Lost Causes" section, "Life in California" subsection, "Land in Lancaster" manila folder, not far from my Bonita file which was stuffed with snapshots, mementos, and the "Dear Frank" letter she'd left me.

As I pulled my newly repaired and painted Volvo into the dusty lot, a buzzard landed on a hand-painted sign that declared cherry juice was for sale at Jerry's Cherry Pit Stop five miles ahead. There was nothing like a long drive down a hot dirt road to make you crave cherry juice. Another cherry juice sign, four-feet by three-feet, stood a few hundred yards down. How dare Jerry put such signs on my private land. I was so mad that I grabbed my gun and loaded in two shells. The bird took off before I approached it.

With the sun beating at my neck and the heat strangling my arms, I aimed my gun and pointed it at the word Jerry on the sign and pulled the trigger, once, then again. The kickback from the two shots was pronounced, but I shouldered them like a pro. I missed the man's name, but the first "Cherry" was mostly air now. That felt great.

Without thinking much, I loaded in two more shells, stepped closer and aimed lower. With one shot I blasted away most of the two-by-four holding the sign up. Sure enough, the sign teetered over. Problem was, it teetered right at me, twisting, falling like an ax blade onto my right foot, covered only by a canvas shoe. I screamed and felt my finger pull the trigger again. I blew away a lot of dirt, the tip of my left shoe, and by the looks of it, perhaps some toes.

I dropped the gun as I toppled and, as luck would have it, I landed on my tailbone on a rock, which caused me to scream again. As I twisted in the hot dirt, seeing blood drip from my shoe and feeling the drumming sting in my foot and back, I threw up. The overwhelming pain was more than anything I had ever experienced at once, and the reaction was all automatic.

What caught me unprepared the most was my instant vision of me as this paunchy slob with a shotgun, reeling in the dust and vomit, Bonitaless. As I writhed and cried, I then envisioned Bonita and me making love in our honeymoon shack, her frizzed-out hair frolicking on her shoulders. Bonita loved me kissing her breasts as she moved her pelvis so dramatically atop me and, damn, the way her body would shake in orgasm and the way she smiled those first few years. I was thin and sure then. How could we have so much and lose it? We had loved each other, the place, our situation, until Fred stoked our desires for more.

After I finished my agony on the baking earth, the buzzard circling overhead, I hobbled to the car and washed my foot with a gallon of windshield washer fluid that I found in the trunk. The sting from the alcohol in it made me nearly throw up again, but that passed quickly when I saw I had all my toes. Some skin and toenails were missing, but the toes were there.

I drove back from the desert with feet that stung with each heartbeat, and I limped into my home, defeated. I wrapped yards and yards of gauze around my naked, scarred foot. The only footwear that would fit after that was a pair of white rabbit slippers with floppy ears that Bonita had once given me for a birthday. I couldn't very well go anywhere like that, including the doctor's office. Besides, I'd probably end up telling him about the gun and the sign, and then I'd feel even more like a koala in a tutu.

Later, as my toes swelled, I thought I'd let my body fight the problem. The body is its own doctor, someone had once told me. I should have known better. My big toe became so massively infected and I was in so much pain, I finally went to the doctor. The big toe had to be amputated. It causes me a funny limp now.

I recall how Mr. Reilly, the "madman," had finally told me he shot those chipmunks because the damn critters carried diseases. He, Howard Hughes, and my mother had their point: Disease is rampant everywhere. If pneumonia, tetanus, and rabies don't get you, the world provides ever-new diseases: Legionnaire's disease, Lyme disease, AIDS. Guns and bullets are nothing compared to the micro invaders trying to destroy us, trying to turn us into one of thirteen ghosts. That's why I shower six times a day now.

Thank god we live in an age where air filtration systems have become a science, where computers and modems let us work from home, and where everything including food and clothing can be delivered through my lockable dog door, a big enough hole. Even if Bonita wanted to come back, she can't because she'd disturb the seal. People carry disease. I realize this seems extreme, and I'm starting to miss everybody, but one has to follow one's beliefs. If global warming continues and Greenland melts, Los Angeles will slip underwater. I've got to do something before then. I just don't know what.

The Old Topanga Incident

You awaken. The sun throws a hue as yellow as a butterfly fish that alights on your bedcover, and you think what a lovely Malibu day. You stayed up far later than usual, tweaking your play, and now it's after eleven a.m. You sit up in bed and feel young again.

Through your window, you see the ocean dramatically below, waves lolling to the beach in front of the seafood restaurant. You laugh because you remember when Tennessee Williams had slept in your guestroom and had woken you up when he'd seen this same view. "Die, you fucking L.A. sunlight!" he'd screamed at the unshaded windows. Tennessee had hated good weather. How horrible he died choking on a bottle cap in his hotel room. Then again, he'd been the master of the dramatic moment.

Lucky, you think, that you have a bit of Tennessee left in your signed first editions of his plays. They stand next to signed books from your friends Dorothy Parker, Somerset Maugham, Lillian Hellman, and others. You flip open the covers to your bed and stand smiling. It's always a joy to wake up with work to do. Today would be a good day to finish your new play, a story of Anton Mesmer and the powers of the mind. You move closer to the window to see the sun through a yellowish haze.

Last night after dinner, you'd watched the news, which said a high-pressure zone had centered over Nevada and Northern

Arizona and had butted up against a low-pressure Southern California coastal. Hot desert air was flowing toward the ocean—the famous Santa Ana winds. But it's November. You look out again at the ocean and think the worst of the summer has passed. The winter rains should start any day. What was the haze—smoke?

You hurry upstairs, move past the Steinway piano that Vladimir Horowitz had played one evening, past the Picasso and the Hirschfeld drawings based on characters from your plays. You zip up the circular staircase to the front door and pass the three theatre seats you installed on the balcony from a torn-down Broadway theatre. You pass a mirror and catch the reflection of a white-haired man in a robe, rounder in the middle than you wished. It doesn't seem like you. It doesn't seem like the guy you remember being, but you're seventy-eight. The many friendly books in the built-in shelves assure you you're fine.

You throw open the tall front doors, a set worthy of King Louis XVI if he were to show up. Across the driveway next to your Mercedes, you see lush green trees sway in the warm breeze—instantly comforting. Nothing's burning nearby. On the ground, colorful lupine, Canterbury bells, and fine daisies move as if from a wave of a Japanese fan. It's why you call it Walden West—a lush and safe two-acre sanctuary fed by the moist ocean breezes.

A particularly loud dove coos. You can't see the bird, but the sunlight, ah, the sunlight, as gorgeous as a red-tail hawk on a thermal. You look into the azure sky and see at last a column of smoke visible far beyond Las Flores Canyon.

Maybe it's in the Valley. You hear a bark and notice your neighbor, a young blond trophy wife who walks her black poodle.

"Good morning!" you say and wave.

"Hey," she says. "Good morning," and she comes down your drive, hair bouncing on her bare shoulders as you walk toward her. Is Nichole her name? Or is it Lisa? You don't remember, but you do what you do with your students, which is simply avoid names altogether.

"Looks like there's a fire," you say.

"Really?" she says, picking up her dog and holding it like a cat.

"Up there," and you point.

She looks and nods. "So that's why I heard sirens earlier. Can the fire spread down here?"

"Doubtful," you say. "Fires like to go uphill, and we're far down. Plus people've been keeping the hillsides trimmed. Too many green things around here." You picture an image from the Rodney King riots a year earlier of liquor stores burning. No liquor stores stand nearby. You will be fine.

She smiles and comes closer.

"The wind is so warm," she says. "It's not from the ocean. Is it from the fire?"

"Santa Anas," you reply. "Raymond Chandler once wrote that they caused fights, and meek little wives felt the edges of carving knives and looked at their husbands' necks. Do you have any carving knives?" You give a wink.

"My husband's neck is just fine," she laughs. "And you think I'm meek? God, no. Only my little puppy here is, aren't you, Dulce?" The dog barks as if on cue. "She's such a brat." The svelte bride kisses the black poodle right on the mouth. Disgusting.

"How sweet," you say.

"My husband reminded me of a play you wrote. You're one of those agnostic writers who gives fundamentalists conniption fits."

"Yes. I hope."

"You don't believe in God? There's something wrong with the religious faithful?"

You can only laugh and shake your head. "No, no. There's definitely a divine spirit around. He helps me write."

Now she laughs and shakes her head as if you're playing with her.

"Truly," you say. "I believe in the creative mind of the universe. We've been created by that intelligence to create and re-create." You realize you sound as silly as Mesmer did explaining animal magnetism to his critics. "I'm a vessel," you offer. "All creative people are. You listen to the sounds of the universe and let them flow through you."

You both remain quiet for a moment, listening. The gentle music of chimes tinkle from the tree where you hung the gift. You also notice the hibiscus at the edge of the driveway has exploded into immense red blooms.

"So you're saying God flowed through you and made you write about doubting God?" she asks. She looks serious.

"If you believe God made everything, then he made disbelievers, agnostics, and scientists, too. He won't mind that I doubt him."

"I know your play," she says. "You resent the faithful. You make fun of God."

"Never," you say. "We only dislike the bullies who think they're God."

"You think Jerry Falwell is a bully?"

"Of course. Isn't this a battle between reason and superstition?"

"I happen to think if you're not faithful, you're missing something," she says. Is that pity on her face?

"I'm quite faithful to my writing. Let me put it this way: I believe in the dignity of every individual mind, and people must spend their lives battling limitation and censorship."

"Dulce needs her walk," she says. "Nice to see you."

"You, too," you say, knowing you've just been dismissed. "Well, if it's going to be a hot day, best to stay inside."

"How true," she says and you part, picking up the newspaper by the front door that has already yellowed in the sun. A color photo of flowers on a sidewalk stands next to the headline "Autopsy Reveals Little on Death of River Phoenix." How sad. A talented actor—only twenty-three. Maybe drugs. You note another, smaller headline "Scars From Firestorm Keep Oakland on Constant Vigil," and you scan it. In a 1991 Oakland Hills fire, many factors worked against containment, including much dry vegetation. You look up at your hillside—perfectly green. It's a gorgeous day minus the pesky fire somewhere. They'll have it out in no time.

You have a quick brunch, an omelet you make for yourself with onions and fresh garlic. An avid bachelor for your whole life, you know how to cook, even though some nights you have a cook come in more for the company than anything—not that you're lonely. You write with a partner and have a rich social life. You have your trysts.

After you clean off your plate, one that you bought on a trip to Mexico, you work at your large desk in your office, using a pen on printed-out pages. You were slow to come to use a computer, but it's a new age and you have the hang of it, a dependable Kaypro computer. You hear more sirens, probably the Malibu fire department going to help in the Valley. You don't notice the sky getting even darker. You want to rewrite five pages. Five pages a day is important.

At around 1:30 p.m., your doorbell rings and rings, and someone pounds on it, too, as if they're being chased by a mob. God damn it—can't people be patient anymore? "Hold your horses," you shout as loudly as you can as you walk up the stairs. Don't people understand this is how working writers work?

You open the door and you see a number of things simultaneously: two firemen in bright yellow rubberized coats stand before you, shouting, "You've got to get out now!" Two hundred yards up the hill is a wall of flame, and the house of the svelte woman with the dog burns brightly as if it were made of gasoline. Flames shoot high. Embers the size of your fist land in the juniper and cypress trees in your yard, on your car, in the driveway.

You stammer, "I need to pack first."

"You can't!" shouts the fireman in front of you, who grabs your arm.

"I need my passport and my play," you say, breaking away and running down the stairs. The fireman follows you shouting,

"Sir, you have to leave now. You only have minutes. This is a monster."

You race down two flights with him clomping behind shouting "Sir!" and you grab the play, the only copy, a clump of pages. You find your passport inside the top drawer, and two bankbooks, too. You clutch and run, returning upwards. Everything you pass you realize you'll never see again—the beautiful wood floors, the art, the china, the crystal vases, the photo albums, the rough drafts, the letters from your mother, and the books inscribed by all your friends. You consider staying there and dying with your things, but the fireman shouts, "Hurry!"

Outside, the driveway swirling in smoke looks covered in gray snow, and the sharp smoky air tears at your throat. You cover your mouth as you cough. The tops of trees where embers landed now burn. Things weren't as green as you'd thought. The fire engine on your street shoots water at the house immediately above yours, whose interior is ablaze. How did you not know this was happening? How could it possibly happen?

You will learn later that the fire had been first reported on the other side of the hill in the morning, near the water tower on Old Topanga Road. The fire spread from one acre to two hundred acres in ten minutes and to a thousand acres in sixty. It's a firestorm with its own eddies and its own convection column that spirals some six miles into the sky. All the while, you had been blissfully editing, completely unaware of your destiny outside your door. The convection column draws oxygen unimpeded from the Pacific, force-feeding the fire with incredible power, three-thousand degrees Fahrenheit. Flame lengths of nearly two-hundred feet will be reported. Three hundred and eighty-eight homes will burn down; 565 firefighters will receive injuries. This is a fire like no other. It will burn your home as easily as a match.

"Thank you!" you shout, even though the firemen are not likely to hear you, and you get in your car; it starts, and you drive. You can feel your heart pound, and you're getting lightheaded. This isn't what someone your age should be doing. You zoom up the drive and down the hill, orange flickering in your rear-view mirror, and hand-grenade-sized embers still falling around you.

You speed up to other cars working their way out, and you shout, "Keep going, keep going." You make it to the Pacific Coast Highway, where a policeman directs you to the left, toward Santa Monica. Where are you headed? What should you do?

You can't quite grasp the loss yet. You're glad you've made it out of there.

You drive as if in a dream. Maybe the firemen will save your house. You have hope. Maybe they're making your street the one they fight back on. Later that afternoon as you watch the news from your hotel room, you recognize the silhouette of your house on fire. You fall back into bed and imagine your life with nothing. Gone are the boxes and boxes of photos in your garage that you'd been meaning to sort. Gone are all your journals you wrote from trips to over one hundred countries. You remember a line from one of them: "Here I am with another freak typewriter with the keys all reversed." People always called you optimistic, but you now realize you can't stay that way. Too much of life is freaky. Life is a bunch of obstacles, and why can't the obstacles stop?

Your writing partner used the words "divine intervention," describing how plays sometimes just came to the two of you. You said, "divine help, you mean."

"That's not the meaning I'm after," he said. "God influences life by intervening in the course of action, positively or negatively. Art is a collaboration with the divine."

"I agree with you in principle, but not the word 'intervention.' I'm being anti-semantic," you quipped.

Now you've just experienced an intervention, a negative one. Fire happened. Divine intervention isn't the term. It's divine indifference.

Two days later when you return to your home, you are a passenger in a car driven by your niece, mid-thirties and steady. You move through the moonscape of your valley. None of the usual landmarks are there, and the whole area is eerily gray. Most trees and telephone poles are bent black fingers pointing accusingly upward. Melted, twisted shells of cars lie here and there in what had been driveways or garages. Blackened foundations stand. Rock black gray, you think.

You turn a particular corner, and you peer. Where your house was is now open to the view; the ocean serenely blue roils below. You get out of the car. A photographer moves in on a blackened post where the front door used to be, and a reporter from the *Times* whom you'd spoken with on the phone waits while a few firemen in yellow douse hot spots on your property. The reporter will want to know what catastrophe means to you. In another era, you might have come up with a quip, such as ashes to ashes, but this is your whole life gone. He will ask, "How you do feel? What was it like?" You wonder now why you agreed to this. You can be a role model. If you can make it through this, others can make it through their tragedies. Everyone has them. But can you make it through this?

"Hello, sir," says the reporter, early forties, long hair, and he shakes your hand as you get out. "How do you feel?"

"Let me look it over first," you say. "Then we'll talk." You spoke this morning to your writing partner. He lives in the Valley with his family, safe in his house, but he's sick. His liver transplant from a few years ago may not be doing well. You consider how you're not doing well, either. Was this God getting back at you two? No, all your neighbors lost their homes, even the faithful.

You don't want to play any parts. You don't want to play. You just want your house back with your stuff.

"Hello, sir," says the photographer, a thin man with a shock of blue hair. "I'm a great fan of your plays."

"Thank you," you say but can't smile. You see a three-story hole near the edge of the driveway, which is the space of your former home. The circular stairs that had taken you downstairs to your rooms has twisted and melted in the heat like an avant-garde statue. You've been liquefied and lost yourself.

"You want to leave?" your niece asks you, and you realize how much like your late sister she appears, long dark hair, beautiful chin. "You don't have to do this in front of these people. It's just a story."

"A story is everything," you say. "Especially mine." You walk forward, proudly, down to where the pool had once been, and you think of the conversation you had with your neighbor about God.

"What are you going to do?" asks the reporter.

"I'll rebuild."

"For it to burn again?"

"I'll rebuild with concrete. I want an unburnable house. It'll be for future playwrights."

"What about all the irreplaceable things you had?"

Are you supposed to cry? You notice a lump in the ashes and realize from the stone headdress that it's your pre-Columbian statue, a blackened fierce warrior. You pick it up, dust it off, and see its arms have fallen off. "Now it really looks pre-Columbian," you mumble. The statue was once Charles Laughton's. You let it drop. You know in that instant your life is over—but not a quick ending like Tennessee's. Yours is the start of a slow erasure.

The reporter stares at you—expects, perhaps, more of your famous optimism, now burnt like the support beams of your house.

You turn to the reporter and say, "I saved our next play from the inferno, and I want to move on it. You look at tomorrow, not yesterday." You hope to say it again and again. You need to believe. You just want to sleep.

A Whisker

"Are you going to like double eagles in fifty years?" said Jean—or was it Joan?

"Seventy-five years old," Bradley whispered, trying to imagine that.

"Won't your birds get wrinkly?" She traced the tattoos on his chest, an eagle above each of his nipples. He had emblazoned these images on himself after he'd started dating Kyla, who had mentioned she had a sailor fantasy.

"I don't know," said Bradley. "It was a stupid thing to do one evening in a fit of feeling happy and sure."

They were in the girl's bedroom in North Hollywood, which had green shag carpeting and a wolf calendar on the wall. Bradley turned over to look at her clock. Now that he was feeling less manic from all the beer, he realized what he had just done was a stupid thing. He shouldn't have come to the party without Kyla where he then met Jean/Joan. Why'd Kyla have to write her thesis tonight? He thought of her now, probably in her black silk nightie in bed. He loved her sense of humor. He loved her smile. Most of all, he loved her breasts, her beautiful pendulous breasts.

"I gotta go," he said, getting out of bed, seeing checker-boards as he stood. He was in no condition to drive yet.

"Are you sure?" the girl said, the covers now off her. She artfully spread her legs.

Maybe he'd stay.

* * *

He stumbled in around four in the morning, waking Kyla as he slipped into bed. Indeed, she slept in her black nightie.

"What time is it?" she asked, curling around his backside, spooning him and wrapping her arm around his naked chest, touching at least one eagle.

"Late. Go to sleep. We'll talk in the morning."

"Was the party good?"

"It was okay. We should sleep," he said.

"Why do you smell?" she asked, sniffing his naked back.

His mind raced. He'd taken a shower there. He shouldn't smell of any sex. "Maybe I spilled a beer on me," he said.

"No, you have a patchouli scent."

He remembered the purple bar in the shower. "Soap," he said.

"On your back?"

His heart sank. How'd she notice such things? It's like when she knew their orange tabby cat had died before they found it under the couch. The cat's pristine blanket, not slept on, had alerted her. His DNA seemed to have that gene miss-ing—the observation gene. And what was he supposed to say now? "I drank too much," he replied. "I stayed there until I felt better."

"And you had to shower? Did you have sex?"

His mouth fell open in awe. How had she made such a con-clusion?

She pulled the covers down, exposing him. "You had sex," she said sternly.

"What makes you think—"

"Your underwear's on backwards."

"Ah," he said seeing how he was an open book. "I acciden-tally slept with someone."

"Accidentally? With who?" she screamed, and then she shoved hard, pushing him out of bed. Only his hands jutting out prevented him from hitting his head.

"That's not nice," he said, feeling that he had just sprained a wrist. He rolled over, his double eagles looking to the sky.

"Who was she?"

"Someone named Jean—I think. You don't know her. She works at Fed Ex Kinkos."

"That's Kinkos Joan. A short girl, red hair?"

He nodded. Kyla seemed to know everyone. She would have found out eventually, he realized. He'd been so stupid. "I'm so so sorry," he said, and then he couldn't see for his tears. He hadn't cried since he was a boy, and now he was curling up outright weeping, and this was so, so, stupid, so sad. "I'm sorry, Kyla."

And now she was crying, too.

"I didn't mean to," he said, crawling back in bed. She pulled the covers up over him, and he cradled her. "I'm so, so sorry," he repeated.

"God damn it," she said between sobs. "Men are such a bad idea."

"It was a mistake," he said.

"Why'd I have to fall for you?"

"We're good together."

"Maybe we need to stop," she said more soberly. "Maybe I should've become a lesbian."

"I—" He knew he should say he loved her, but they never said that to each other. It seemed too silly, and now it would seem too false. She'd know. "It'll never happen again, I promise."

That's when she pushed him out of the bed again. "I want you out today."

He spent the rest of the night on the couch. He didn't think he could fall asleep, but all his drinking and sex must have worn him out. When he awoke, he found a note on the kitchen counter. "Bradley: Get out today. No love, Kyla."

How could she afford to kick him out? He paid half of everything and bought most of the groceries. Still, when she made her mind up about something, that was it. He knew Kyla would never want him back. He called his brother, Vinson, and told him what had happened.

"How could you do that?" said Vinson, incredulous. "Kyla is so nice."

"Do you know Kinkos Joan?"

"The redhead? She's hot. You did it with her?"

"Yeah."

"Lucky bastard."

Vinson gave him a few leads for a place to rent, half-heartedly saying Bradley could stay with him for a few days.

"Maybe I'll find something today," said Bradley. He did: an apartment in Hollywood that was, as the landlord said, "Adjacent to Beverly Hills Adjacent." A one-bedroom unit, it came with a refrigerator and it had hardwood floors. He loved the place, so he forked over first and last month's rent. As a computer programmer specializing in games, he made good money.

Bradley moved that day. Vinson, two years younger at twenty-three, came with a rented U-Haul van, and the two of them wrestled out Bradley's desk, his double bed that had been in storage in the garage, his computer, clothes, and other items, nearly filling the van.

That afternoon, lying alone on his naked mattress in his new apartment, Bradley felt he could be in Abu Dhabi. Everything was strange. The dome light on his ceiling was strange. The vegetable color of the wall was strange. So, too, were the tears emerging from his eyes once again. Why had he slept with Joan—what was the deal with that? Even when he'd been drunk, part of him knew he shouldn't follow through.

Bradley now stared at his green walls. They were the color of artichokes. Kyla had cooked him artichokes. She had even made hollandaise sauce for him from scratch for the artichokes.

"I love this," he'd said the first time, dipping a leaf into the sauce.

"You really do?"

"It's the best I've ever had." Never mind he'd never eaten it before.

"You're the best!" She had kissed him deeply, put her hands under his shirt. They'd made love on the floor. She was the best.

"You're sweeter than the cat," she'd said. And she had loved that cat.

He stood. He realized she had been his twin flame. Why had he messed up something so special?

He paced on the hardwood floor. If Kyla had not caught him, would he have been able to live with his lie? What had made him think he could get away with sleeping with another woman?

He hated these questions. All he knew was the last few months with Kyla studying hadn't been fun. Fun? Was this fun?

He moved into the kitchen, glared at all the boxes, and opened the refrigerator. It was chilled and empty. He shut it, grabbed his cell phone, and pressed the speed-dial for Kyla, but her Caller ID obviously betrayed him. She didn't answer. In another year, some other guy would be with her. Without even thinking, he kicked one of his boxes hard. Glass shattered and tinkled.

Pissed, he grabbed the box of broken glassware and marched to his back door. He threw the box unopened into the dumpster in the alley. A dark streak raced by, an animal of some sort. As Bradley entered the kitchen, a black cat with a white tummy sat on its haunches as if it owned the place. The cat brushed against his leg, back and forth like a fuzzy shark with white whiskers. One whisker was black.

"You lost, little guy?"

The cat looked up at him and nodded.

"How would you like to live here? How would you like the name Mr. Moonpie?" The cat nodded again. Later Bradley would learn the cat was female, but by then Mr. Moonpie was just too good a name.

He returned to his bedroom, sat back on his bed, and as simply as gravity pulls at the moon, he knew he had to get Kyla back.

He wanted her so much, he grabbed his phone again from his pocket and text-messaged her: "i luv u, and i'm sorry, i m so dum sometimes. i don't know y i did what i did. have me back." When he received no response, he set up his computer and tried e-mailing her. He attached a photo of himself at the beach that she took where his tattoos had shown prominently. His tattoos, as Joan had pointed out, would last into his old age. Kyla should realize his commitment to her in tattoos.

Still no response. What could he do?

* * *

A week later with still no word from Kyla, Bradley bought a large Hallmark card with roses on the front and a poem inside about the magic of love being so magical. Mr. Moonpie jumped on top of his desk as Bradley wrote underneath the poem: "Kyla, we have something special, as strong as gum stuck under a seat. I'm sorry about what happened."

The cat walked on the card back and forth, purring. "Mr. Moonpie, stop. I've got to write this," and Bradley continued with his note: "It's not that I mind you getting a degree. Heck, I have a degree, but we had so little time for each other. We were down to sex twice a week, like some old married couple. I should have been patient because you're graduating this month. Will you have me back? How about we celebrate with a pool of margaritas?"

Bradley considered. "Should I add a poem of my own?" he asked the cat. The cat stared at the card. Bradley took it as a yes, he should write a poem.

"Roses are red, violets are blue, have me back because I love you."

Mr. Moonpie went into convulsions, sticking her tongue out and coughing. She threw up a big black ball of hair and all sorts of brown liquid right onto the card.

"Mr. Moonpie!" Staring at the dark gelatinous mass and coffee-like liquid, Bradley realized he had to throw the whole card away now. There went $3.98.

As he carefully lifted the card to dispose of it and prevent the liquid pouring onto his desk, the only word not covered by the upchuck was the word "pool." He remembered Kyla by a pool. He'd taken her to Catalina Island, an hour's speedboat ride from L.A. They had a dumpy little hotel room at the Zane Grey that had a breathtaking view, and all he wanted was her naked. She wanted to commune with her *Cosmo*. At one point by the pool as she was reading her magazine, he plunked next to her and said, "How about we return to the room for a rendezvous?" He moved his eyebrows up and down, trying to be cute.

She slapped his arm playfully. "You think of a vacation as sex, sex, sex. I think of it as doing this, reading stupid junk, relaxing by the pool."

"So you don't like, you know, to be with me?" he'd said.

"Men count the number of days since having sex, and if they think there's a problem in the relationship, they cite the number. Don't give me the number now. I'm reading *Cosmo*."

Bradley now did not want more days to elapse. He saw this destroyed card in the trash not as a disaster but as the cat trying to help him. This card would have been a mistake. The cat was suggesting he could do better.

Bradley made a new card by folding thick resume paper into quarters. On the front, he glued a photo of Kyla kissing him. He pulled out his *Norton Anthology of Poetry* from his box of books—he still had a lot of unpacking to do—and he found a sonnet, "Shall I compare thee to a summer's day?" by William Shakespeare. He paraphrased it, saying that she was like a summer's day, temperate and reasonable, not like the winds of May. Her devotion was beyond measure, even by the crazy nature of a man, and as long as he could breathe or see, she made his life worth living. One line of Shakespeare's he didn't use: "Sometime too hot the eye of heaven shines."

"Okay?" he said to the cat. Mr. Moonpie nodded, grooming itself with its front paw. A whisker fell into the card.

He mailed the card, keeping the whisker inside and rubbing his double eagles for good luck. Two days later Kyla was at his door in a short little white top and tight jeans. She jumped on top of him and within minutes they were making wild love, her breasts untamed again, wild horses finding Monument Valley. She soon moved in, and later they both came down with herpes thanks to Kinkos Jean—or was it Joan? Sometime too hot the eye of heaven shines.

Months
And
Seasons

I t'd been nearly three weeks, and his hand was almost healed. The bandages were gone and the fingers worked, but Cody did not want to go to a party. His former college roommate, Henderson from Hawaii, insisted. They had been on the same film together and, as Henderson said, "It's what we toil for—the cast-and-crew party."

Henderson picked him up at his apartment on Beachwood Drive promptly at seven, and they drove to Monrovia, near where the film had been shot. The party was for *The Old Movie House Horror*, a parody of *The Phantom of the Opera*. It focused on a man who owned a pool cleaning service; he'd been burned by pool acid and was living in a secret basement under an old movie theatre that was now a Gap store.

Several minutes into the drive, as they were circling around Lake Hollywood, Henderson said, "You got to lighten up, guy."

"I'm just not a good friend to be with," said Cody.

"Of course you are. You're just upset about what's-her-name."

"Her name was Tasha. Names are important."

"She wasn't right for you," said Henderson. "And since when could you fall for a sorority girl? Aren't you a little beyond that?" Tasha had been an extra on the previous film they'd worked, *Babe with a Blade,* about a woman who eats the wrong sushi on a first date and transforms into a vampire trained to kill like a Viking priestess. She's brought to Iraq to do ultimate good. The extras were for a skinny-dipping scene.

"The heart has its own reasons," said Cody.

"Don't make me puke. Besides, you're the one who says monogamy doesn't work biologically. Men need to spread their seed while women make just a few kids and stop needing sex. You said that."

"I had a biology class at the time."

"So isn't it still the truth?"

"Haven't you had the need to connect? I mean, really connect beyond sex?"

"Right," said Henderson with a smirk.

"This is pointless," said Cody. "I mean, the movie we made —who's it for? Teenagers? If it's for teenagers, what teenager has seen *The Phantom of the Opera*—the original movie or the expensive play? How will they get the parody?"

"Who cares? We were paid. You didn't like lighting those topless young women, helpless in the showers?"

"Yeah, that was... I was going for chiaroscuro."

Henderson laughed. "Sometimes you talk just like the English major you were."

"Except that's art-major talk."

"Like I said, lighten up."

Cody looked at his hand, flexing some of his fingers. He last saw Tasha at a microbrewery in Westwood. She'd invited him there only to tell him they were over. He left so angrily that he punched a stop sign and hurt his hand. Nothing was broken, but it had become sore and swollen and he had had difficulty working with it—but he managed.

"You still promise that after an hour if I don't like the party, you'll drive me back?" said Cody.

"Absolutely," said Henderson. "But you have to promise you'll converse with at least three women. A conversation is at least four back-and-forth sets of dialogue."

"Oh, and you'll be documenting?"

"I trust you."

"I'm not ready, and I don't like the pushing. The fact is, the right woman won't be at a cast party. The woman I'll love won't be in films."

"Don't make me laugh. The woman you'll love will catch you off-guard as they always have and— What was that thing with names last week?"

"Names have power."

"So she has to be named what? Walnut or Juniper?"

"No, not trees. Look how you mix things up. It's months or seasons."

"For crying out loud," said Henderson.

"Only my girlfriends May and Summer have really understood me. I need to match one of them."

"They were college flings!"

"I was insane to leave either. You only get so many chances in this life. It's like heartbeats—you only get so many."

"We have two hot women on the crew, Rose and Brandy. What's wrong with them?"

"Names for a flower or liquor? Not right."

"Then don't ask anyone her name. Get to know her for her. As you always say, women are human beings."

"Don't mock me. I'm talking about destiny. It may seem stupid to you but—"

"Destiny is spreading your sperm to more places than a napkin. We're not leaving until you have at least three full conversations."

Cody rolled his eyes. His old roommate still didn't see there were powers beyond mere biological drive. The universe was a mysterious place.

"So you're agreed? Three conversations with three different women?"

Cody nodded. He didn't tell Henderson he hoped he could scrounge up another job at the party. That's all he was really there for. As he thought about it, though, he was tiring of this seat-of-your-pants lifestyle—good pay for a short time, then it was a race to find another dumb movie at less-than-union scale. Lately as he slept, too, he literally dreamed he was still at work, dragging cables, calculating amperage, plugging things in. There had to be better things.

Henderson drove high into the Monrovia hills. The party, at the home of one of the producers, had a panoramic view of Monrovia below. They strode into the courtyard, which featured a Spanish-tiled fountain with spitting frogs and real lily pads. The area was larger than his whole apartment. Inside the house, the foyer was made of slate, and the spacious living room offered dark earth tones, a white baby grand piano, a large bookcase, and what appeared to be a flattened elephant's head on a wall. Near it, a stone fireplace snapped with burning logs.

As soon as they entered the living room, Henderson pointed through the French doors to the back yard and the pool. Near the doors stood Brandy, one of the hot women. She wore a black dress with a low-cut neckline and necklace, and her posture accentuated her graceful curves. She could be one of the female statues in the bookcase.

"Let's meet up in a half hour," said Henderson, taking off.

Feeling awkward, Cody moved to the wall, examined the elephant's head and its giant ears and saw the thing was carved from wood. The trunk, which nearly stretched to the floor, had every believable crease.

"It's amazing, isn't it?" Cody turned to see Roger Spillman, a dapper man in his seventies with shock-white hair, the man who owned the house.

"It's so real," Cody said.

"I found the most amazing artist in Thailand. He makes very little doing stuff like this. It cost more to ship it than I paid him for the piece."

Cody knew that Spillman first made money in the sixties and seventies on the drive-in and rural movie markets, films with mutants from the deep that preyed on cheerleaders or roller-skating carhops and a film about buxom airline stewardesses in jail. He kept expenses low and profits high. He seemed to have adapted to the new DVD crowd.

"I've never understood artists," said Cody. "It's as if they have some special line to another power. How did this guy know what to chip away?"

"I happened to be lost, looking for the Madison Steakhouse in Bangkok," said Spillman. "And I went down a street of artisans and came across this. Coincidence."

Cody nodded, wondering why anyone would want to eat at an American-sounding steakhouse in Thailand.

"I look at my life," said Spillman, peering deeply at the elephant's head, maybe even through it, "and I wonder how it could possibly all be coincidence. It can't. Something has guided me."

Something guided him into soft porn? Cody didn't know what to say to that, but he'd never spoken to Spillman before. This was perhaps his best chance to make an impression, maybe even get another job. "Sometimes what's coincidental, isn't," said Cody. "There are powers beyond us."

"So true," said Spillman, raising his glass in a toast. "To powers beyond us!" Cody had no drink to toast with, so he mimed one. With that, Spillman saw an older couple entering, said "Excuse me," and left. Cody winced. Should he have said something else? Except he'd said what was true—Cody believed in belief. He was like the late Danish philosopher Soren Kirkegaard, except he was working in America on a movie set with giant power cables and topless women. He and Soren were awed by faith. Cody couldn't explain why he believed names were important, for example, but they were. He just knew. There were things beyond science.

Cody realized, too, he'd had a full conversation with Spillman, at least four back-and-forth sets of dialogue. That had to count for something. He wouldn't tell Henderson it wasn't with a woman. Now he needed just two more conversations.

A white-jacketed server, a young woman with her dark hair in a bun, came up with champagne flutes. "Champagne?" she said, smiling.

"Is it Californian?" he asked, not knowing why. He felt stupid instantly. This was another reason he hated parties. He didn't know what to say to women at first. "I'm sorry," he said, "I don't know why I said that because I don't drink champagne. It gives me a headache." She nodded and walked off.

That didn't count as a conversation. He glanced out back for Henderson. He didn't see him or Brandy. He headed outside.

Out back, a cobalt-tiled pool hugged a hillside covered in ice plants and statuary. Around the pool stood many of the guests, most of them dressed far better than when they'd been on set.

"Hey, hand looks good," said a young woman in a red gown coming up to him. Cody didn't recognize her at first, then realized it was one of the women from accounting, the one who delivered checks.

"Hey, Jane," he said. How much more plain could you get for a name than hers?

"How's it feel, dude?" she said.

"Fine, thanks." He moved some of his fingers. "So do you have another movie job lined up?"

"They're keeping me on through post-production to help out in the office," she said. "Spillman gave me another few months. Then I think I'll go back to UCLA."

He nodded, then realized they needed one more set of exchanges to qualify for Henderson's minimum. "You didn't grow up in L.A., right?"

"No," she said. "Las Vegas."

Yikes, he thought to himself. A Las Vegas upbringing must have warped her. "Nice seeing you. I've got to find Henderson," he said. She looked surprised, but the conversation took more out of him than he'd expected. He sensed she was searching for that one person, and Cody didn't want to be it. She had the wrong name. He didn't want to waste Jane's time.

He spotted Henderson with Brandy and the other hot woman, Rose. Henderson had put on his black-framed glasses, which had plain glass. The guy didn't need them to see. He wore them often because it made him look like the late actor Peter Sellers, who, Cody thought, wasn't particularly handsome. Besides, who knew bygone stars anyway? You're a celebrity one day, then you're black-and-white on Turner Classics the next. Then the film stock disintegrated and you were dust, unless the American Film Institute revived you.

Brandy laughed, and Rose joined in, to Henderson's delight. What had he said? Henderson wasn't particularly witty. Sure, they'd been in the same frat house at the University of Rochester and traveled to Italy together, had some laughing Mediterranean times. Henderson might know Heidegger's philosophy as it related to *The Simpsons*—Lisa as *dasein,* Homer as the deliverer of ordinary truths that eluded us—but the guy wasn't witty. Yet there was Henderson with his fake glasses and strong confidence attracting the women. He wasn't out to be a couple as Cody had always wanted for himself. The irony made him want to punch Henderson.

He started walking toward Henderson when he heard a scream, and right to his side, a woman was falling, perhaps tripping on a crack in the terracing. He instinctively reached out to help, and he grabbed her by her outstretched arms before she hit. As he clutched her, the red wine in her plastic cup found his white pants at his crotch. The area was now wet and cabernet-colored.

"Thank you," she said, and she saw his pants. "Oh, I'm so sorry." She reached with her party napkin to wipe the splotch when she pulled back awkwardly. "I'm sorry. You better do it." She handed him the napkin.

"Thanks," he said.

"No, thank you. I could have been hurt or scraped up. I'm not used to heels." Her low-heeled silver shoes went well with her black silk pants and turquoise top.

"No problem. At least you're okay." Cody wiped more. "Wine'll come out with carpet cleaner spray," he said. "Resolve. I have some at home."

"It's grape juice, actually," she said in a lilting accent. "Sorry, but if you give it to me, I can have it dry cleaned."

What was he supposed to do? Take off his pants right there? He shook his head and said, "Thanks anyway." He now noticed that the blue cocktail napkin he'd used for swabbing the wet wine had added a cobalt color to his pants. He looked like a clown.

She, on the other hand, striking, lithe, sure of herself, stood before him with concern and held out her hand. "My name's August."

"August?" he said astounded, glancing at her from head to toe. "Really? That's your name? Unusual."

"August Strindberg, no?" she said. "A Swedish playwright."

"Right," he said. "Sweden. Is that where you're from?"

"Buffalo, New York, actually."

"Hey, I'm from Rochester—just an hour away. Except your accent isn't—"

"My mother's Irish. I must have absorbed—"

"Ah," said Cody, taking her hand and shaking it. "My name's Cody." How lucky was his night?

"Anyway, I'm sorry about the spill," she said.

"People trip all the time. May I get you something more to drink?"

"No, thanks. Actually, I'm going outside for a quick—" She pantomimed smoking a joint. "Want to join me?"

Normally he wouldn't. He smoked nothing, yet he hadn't expected to meet August. This was fate. He'd go with August anywhere.

Away from the pool, high in the Monrovia hills overlooking the 210 Freeway and under a private gazebo by the stairs, they sat. He took a hit and coughed so hard, he thought he'd throw up.

"You okay?"

"Yeah, sure," though he wasn't. "So what did you do on this film?"

"Script supervisor," she said. He nodded. Now she looked familiar. "And you?"

"Best Boy," he replied.

She started laughing hard. "Are you joking?"

"No, why?"

"What's a Best Boy?"

"An electrician, assistant to the gaffer—kind of like a manager. The person who makes sure no one's electrocuted."

"That's important."

"Damn straight. If a light's ungrounded, and you touch it, zap. People can get electrocuted, too, when you mix lights and water, like in those shower scenes—gotta be careful. If you calculate wrong, circuits burn. Lights can explode if there's not a proper neutral."

"How horrible."

"Absolutely. It's a death trap out there. Watts, you know, equals volts times amps, and if you have, say, three one-K lights—one thousand watt units—" He stopped when he realized she was laughing, and it all suddenly seemed funny to him, too.

"Electricity does sound bizarre—but it's all about math," he said. "Rules of physics."

"Good stuff," she said. He wasn't sure if she was referring to the weed or to physics.

"I guess so," he replied. He glanced down to notice that the cut of her turquoise top revealed a hint of black lacy bra, one that pushed her two breasts together so they touched. He'd love to be her bra.

"Funny we've never met until now." She offered the joint to him again and he took it.

"You believe in coincidence?" he asked.

"Sometimes. Not like there's an entity looking at six billion people on this planet guiding us into anything, making us do shit. But maybe we have a dab of Harry Potter, you know? A little magic beyond electrons becoming amps or volts, whatever."

He nodded. "Did you see that elephant's head in there?"

"I think it's horrible. To kill a perfectly good elephant to—"

"No, it's all wood. It's carved," he said, laughing again.

"No shit? Well then, that's different." Her grin could carry tanks over the Euphrates.

They chatted and smoked, then smoked a little more until Cody heard a large gurgle. August looked him straight in the eyes, smiling. She didn't have to say a thing because Cody knew. "That's your gurgle," he said. "You're hungry."

"Yep, my biology," she said. "I hear there're crab legs and lobster bisque. You like that?"

"Of course." He didn't like seafood in particular, but he stood. Right now he'd eat week-old sushi and sand crabs, and he took her hand. She squeezed his hand gently back, which he took as a sign. Like two one-thousand-amp fireflies, if little bugs could have that much power, he and August were meant to double their glow.

As they walked into the courtyard, they approached the fountain with its spitting frogs, and the moment seemed simply perfect. He approached her face surely. They kissed. She threw her head back and laughed to the sky like the goddess Demeter causing water to flow. He kissed her again. He could be the son of Zeus.

"You want to come to my place later, and I can wash your pants?" she asked.

"Sure," he said, "except Henderson drove me here."

"I'll drive you back home whenever," she said.

He smiled so hard, he tilted his head back and noticed the North Star. There indeed was something magical about this place.

When they walked in hand-in-hand, Henderson was near the door with some guy talking about hockey and the feel of the puck under the control of your stick. When Henderson saw them, he smiled, perhaps in amazement. "Hey, guy," he said to Cody. "Did you see that you're peeing a rainbow?"

Cody looked down at his pants again, grinned and nodded.

"You ready to go?" Henderson asked.

"She's taking me back," said Cody pointing to August.

"Good to hear," said Henderson. "Have we met?"

August frowned slightly as if surprised, then said, "My name's August. We met at lunch one day on the set. I usually wear plainer clothes."

"Ah, August," he said, now noticing the depth of her neckline, too. "That's right. Nice to meet you again, August." He winked at Cody, clearly happy for him. Or was Henderson toying with him like some goofy frat brother?

Cody and August approached the buffet choices on the center island and the black granite-topped kitchen counters, peering at the selection of food. A mountain of shrimp as white as Utah snow stood next to a railroad yard of succulent crab legs. Cocktail sauce in a bowl promised zing. Steam trays of potatoes, green beans with garlic, and lobster bisque all suggested pure pleasure. August licked her lips and excused herself to go to the bathroom.

"I'll wait here for you," said Cody. She kissed him fully on the mouth again, then ran off down the hallway. She passed Jane, coming from the bathroom, who said something like, "Hey, Beca."

Cody frowned.

Jane approached the buffet area. She looked at Cody again warily.

"Better than Vegas?" he asked, pointing to all the food.

"Vegas can be as good as this," she said. "Even better."

"That girl you passed just now," he said, "you deliver her paycheck each week, right? What did you just call her?"

Jane turned to look down the hallway, but August was gone. Even so, Jane nodded. "Rebecca, you mean?"

"Rebecca? She told me her name was August."

"I don't know. Her middle initial is A, but I thought it was for Ann. Rebecca Ann."

At that moment, Cody saw Henderson across the room talking with Roger Spillman at the piano. Spillman was playing some light jazz while chatting with Henderson. Goddamn it, Cody realized: Henderson knew. Cody didn't care about etiquette. He marched right over as Spillman was saying, "...which appeal to me most—stories of treachery and the like—things people really go through. I'm proud of distributing those foreign films."

"Excuse me, sir, but I need to talk to Henderson," said Cody.

"Go ahead," Spillman said.

Cody and Henderson stepped just a few feet out of the way when Cody said, "You told her, didn't you, about my need for names?"

"What?"

"Rebecca, isn't that her name?"

"August?" said Henderson with some amusement.

"Did you tell her about my notion of months and seasons?"

"Could be," he said. "She wanted to meet you. Is there a crime in that?"

"Are you talking about Rebecca?" said Spillman from the piano.

"Yes," said Cody.

"A very dependable girl," said Spillman. "I've used her on my last five films."

"Is she from Buffalo, New York?" asked Cody.

"Mankato, Minnesota, I believe," said Spillman. "A farm girl. Stern Swedish parents right out of a Bergman film."

Cody looked up to see August/Rebecca standing some distance away, looking sheepish and ashamed. Spillman waved her over. She looked at the front door as if planning her escape, but she stepped up to them.

"So, you heard," she said.

"I don't get it," said Cody. "People know you here as Rebecca."

"I didn't know how to meet you. One day Henderson told me how."

As he looked at Henderson and Spillman, their smiles seemed to find such amusement that his stomach knotted.

Cody couldn't stand it—maybe he shouldn't have smoked—and he hurried for the door that Rebecca had considered. He didn't look back.

When he was by the fountain, he heard Rebecca say, steps behind him, "Come on. Is it wrong to want to meet you?"

"You were playing with my belief system," he said and faced her.

"You have a sense of humor, don't you?" she said. "Or is everything serious?"

As he looked down at the frogs spitting, he noticed his pants again, red and blue at his crotch. She had a point.

"Sometimes you can't wait for fate," she added. She held out her hand.

Henderson entered the courtyard, and Cody pointed at him accusingly. "I'm pissed at you for doing this!"

"You should be thanking me."

"My whole body is angry," said Cody. "I can't just turn that off."

Henderson nodded as if he knew and turned back into the house.

Rebecca—that was her name, names were important—again held out her hand.

"I don't know," said Cody.

She reached forward, and a spark of static electricity went from her forefinger to his. It startled him, and he realized the ember of energy could not be accidental. It was a sign. After all, electricity was a special power, his field.

"Do you happen to know the meaning of your name?" he asked. He wondered if he'd know her tomorrow let alone months or seasons from now.

Before her answer, he took her hand. He wanted her. In the fountain, the spitting frogs paused as if to listen.

The
Wind
Just
Right

The note from Mr. Bertoni, the swimming director, instructed Tutti to be at the beach at 11 a.m. She wouldn't be leading a hike after all, but probably helping Mr. Bertoni as a lifeguard. That sucked. This whole summer had sucked so far. Her parents were divorcing, and the only thing they'd agreed on was when they'd forced her to take the job at this camp. Camp was fun at thirteen—stupid at seventeen. Besides, Tutti knew why she was here. She'd been in the way.

"Over here, Tutti," called Mr. Bertoni on the beach. The light wind coming off the water ruffled his longish graying hair. As the counselor in charge of swimming at Camp Elsa Linson in Northern Minnesota, he was perhaps the busiest person at the camp. The first classes started at nine each morning and went till five.

Mr. Bertoni knelt down next to a seven-year-old girl in a blue suit whose arms were crossed, and the girl glared into the sand. Tutti thought this paunchy kid might punch him in the face at any second. Tutti felt something similar. She didn't want to be here, either.

A bird cawed above, and Tutti cranked her head up. A crow flew into the trees beyond the beach. The woods looked particularly dark this morning. Between the beach and the woods stood a narrow swamp where lily pads and cattails grew. The long stems waved in the cool breeze.

"I don't want to swim!" said the little girl.

"It's okay, Anna," said Mr. Bertoni to the girl. "Tutti will help you."

Tutti, dressed in her red one-piece suit and wearing a Minnesota Twins sweatshirt, tried to get Mr. Bertoni's attention with her own look that said, "No way." Tutti knew nothing about teaching. She had her Junior Lifesaving card, true, but she had no experience teaching and no desire to teach.

"Please," said young Anna, pleading, echoing Tutti's feeling. "I'll do anything else. Make me clean up bear poop or something." The girl stared at the ground.

"You'll be fine."

Anna shook her head, kicking at the sand. "My grandpa always calls me a rock. I'm going to sink."

Mr. Bertoni smiled. "I think he meant you're reliable. Tutti will help you get used to the water."

The girl glowered at Tutti, and Tutti knew the girl probably would sink. Maybe they could sink together, and then there'd be no more worries, no more feeling rotten like the toy goose her dog used to thrash around until stuffing went flying, snow on the dark carpet.

"Mr. Bertoni?" said Tutti. "I think I'm here by mistake. I volunteered for hiking."

"I asked for you. I've seen you swim here every summer since you were a little girl. You're a sunfish. You'll be fine."

No, she wouldn't. "Can I talk to you about something?" She meant alone.

"Stay here, Anna," he told the girl. "One second."

He indicated to Tutti to follow him some steps down the beach. About twenty feet away, he stopped. "What?" he asked.

"I can't teach her."

"Why not?"

"You're mistaking me for someone else. I've never taught and—"

"You're the right person."

"She doesn't want to be taught."

They looked at Anna who stared fiercely at them. "That's your challenge," Mr. Bertoni said.

"But I don't want a challenge."

"You wanted to be a counselor, I thought."

Her stomach turned. "But I've never taught anything. I'm good for...." She left her mother's word, "nothing," alone.

Mr. Bertoni smiled and waved Anna over. She came, re-crossing her arms. "Anna, Tutti is only going to get you used to the water. You're not going to swim today, understand?"

Anna stepped back, frightened as if Tutti were some Grizzly. Tutti shook her head. This kid was going to be horrible.

"Tutti," said Mr. Bertoni. "As you can see, Anna isn't sure about the water. As the Zen master says, to get to China, you have to take the first step."

Tutti frowned. China? What Zen master? Zen?

"The first step for you," Mr. Bertoni told Tutti, "is just show Anna that the lake is like a talking candle. It can be your friend."

A talking candle? This guy was off his rocker.

Anna stepped forward aggressively. "My brother says the fish in the lake are just like my goldfish—they poop and pee in the water. I'm not stepping into that."

"Your parents told me they need you to learn for your own safety," said Mr. Bertoni. "After all, Minnesota has over ten thousand lakes."

"And lots of streams and swimming pools," added Tutti, who then noticed Anna zapping her with laser eyes. If Tutti had been a talking candle, she'd be a puddle of wax now.

"Okay, you two," said Mr. Bertoni. "Stay in the shallows and have fun. I've got to watch the junior sharks swim a mile." Mr. Bertoni stepped on the dock and waved toward the group of "junior shark" girls near the dock's end, built in the shape of a football goal. Kids would swim between the arms. Forty-four times back and forth equaled a mile. Tutti had done it every year for the last five years.

"Let's just walk into the water a little bit," said Tutti.

"No," said Anna.

"How about we walk in just up to our ankles?"

"I don't like my feet to get wet."

"To be frightened of the water," said Tutti. "That's like being afraid of ice cream or watermelon."

"Can ice cream kill you?" said Anna.

"Water on your ankles won't kill you."

"You can't make me," said Anna. "I'm going back to my cabin," and she started walking.

"Mr. Bertoni?" said Tutti loudly, but he was out of range.

Even so, that made Anna pause. "He can't hear you," said Anna.

Tutti lurched toward Anna. She wanted to grab the damn kid and just throw her in. Anna gave a short scream and fell down.

Tutti glanced at the dock. Mr. Bertoni was busy and didn't seem to have heard the scream. Gritting her teeth like her father, she said, "Listen, damn it. Let's just start. We'll go in the shallow part and—"

Anna had tears in her eyes. "I'm going to drown," she said as a quiet fact.

"No, you're not."

Anna only shook her head, faster, harder, more frightened.

Tutti flashed on the fear she herself had felt months earlier when she'd heard her parents fighting downstairs, then a glass crashing. "Don't be so dramatic," her father had shouted, and her mother screamed, "I want you out now!" When she heard the front door slam, Tutti pulled a pillow over her head and cried.

"Okay," Tutti now said. "I'm not going to throw you in the water, if that's what you're worried about. We'll barely walk in."

"I don't want to walk in."

Tutti looked at the trees, wondering again what the hell a Zen master was. She watched the crow take off. It now seemed a graceful bird. "You know why I like the water?" said Tutti, turning back. "I love the water because it makes cool patterns. You know what a pattern is?"

"No."

"A pattern is a design," said Tutti, but the girl still looked puzzled. "It's like the way wallpaper can look, or clothing. Look out there on the lake, and if you look hard enough, you can see waves, one after the other. That's a design." The girl looked, and Tutti smiled seeing that Anna at last had listened to something. "If we go to the water's edge but don't step in, and if we look *really* closely at the water, you'll see teeny tiny waves like lines that repeat. You ever notice that in the water?"

Anna shook her head. "James at school has a line under his chin. That's where he fell on a rock from a wall."

"That's a scar," said Tutti. "This is different. Want to see lines in the water?"

Anna said nothing, still looking doubtful. Tutti gently took her arm, and they stepped forward to the water's edge.

"Do you feel the breeze from the lake?" said Tutti, and Anna nodded. "Well, that breeze is what makes the waves and the lines on the water. You have to get closer to see the lines. Let me show you." Tutti walked into the water, but the girl did not follow. All right, so maybe this wasn't going to work.

"There's another way to make patterns, too," said Tutti, "and that's with a rock. If you drop a rock in, it'll make little circles on the water—a pattern." Tutti stepped into the water, reached down, and found a stone in the sand. She held the stone high over the water, then let it drop. It blurped in, and little rings on the surface radiated out like an animation of radio waves. "Isn't that neat?" said Tutti.

Anna nodded. She walked right into the water, leaned down, stuck her hand in the water, and came up with her own rock. She let it go. She watched the pattern intently.

Tutti smiled. The kid had walked in, forgetting her fear. "Look at the pattern your feet make when you stomp your foot down hard," said Tutti, stomping and creating a splash. "See, the wave pattern is sharper."

Anna did the same, but, being short, her splash hit her face. Anna froze. "That water is wet," said Anna, as if it were news. "Kind of cold. What about all the fish?"

"They're a ways out there," said Tutti. "They're no fish in the shallows. Anyway, fish don't like people and stay away."

Anna stomped another time, making a bigger splash and giggling.

Next came squishing sand between their toes. They walked a foot into the lake and ground their feet in and wiggled their toes. "It feels like throw-up," said Anna.

"Throw-up between your toes?"

Anna smiled eagerly, a rebel. Soon they splashed each other with karate chops. It took a week of such things, never venturing more than a few feet into the shallows, but then Anna trusted Tutti enough for Tutti to hold Anna on top of the water, floating. In another week, Anna was dog paddling on her own.

"Let's go out farther," said Tutti.

Anna stopped swimming and stood in the water up to her waist. She shook her head vigorously.

"You're not scared of the deep, are you?"

Anna said nothing. She clearly was.

"You're it," said Tutti, tagging Anna on the shoulder. Tutti swam parallel to the shore, not going deeper, and she swam slowly enough for Anna to catch her. When Anna tagged her, Tutti shouted, "Not fair!"

"I'm faster than you," said Anna.

"Oh, yeah?" Tutti gave a mini-leap toward Anna, who took off swimming.

"If you tag the dock, you're safe," said Tutti.

Anna giggled and dog paddled furiously, aiming for the dock in the deep water.

"Not fair, you're too fast!" said Tutti, which made Anna laugh with joy. Anna touched the dock and shouted, "Safe! Can't get me."

"Look at that, Anna. You're in the deep part."

Anna looked frightened for a second, and then beamed. A couple of the junior sharks standing above her on the dock said, "Good work. Hurray!"

"You're a sunfish," said Tutti, and Anna looked even prouder.

Tutti heard a caw and noticed the crow glide above, and watching its sureness, she knew she'd make it through her parents' divorce. They'd each written her lately how much they loved her, how much they missed her, and that marriage—sometimes things don't go the way you expect.

The crow landed on a branch of the closest tree, and Tutti couldn't help but notice the leaves on that tree, fluttering like junior sharks cheering her on.

Breaking Water

M errill stood on top of the white roof of funny the little red car. The car could have been a Mini Cooper with a lot of tall clowns in it, but rather it was another brand of vehicle, empty, floating, moving and sinking in a river edged by trees and steep banks. The movement made her dizzy. She froze at the sound of a waterfall. Oh-oh. If she didn't drown, she'd fall to her death. Life was over at thirty-six.

Shattering glass startled her, and she felt herself lurch up, heart beating quickly. She sat in a bed. Her sister Stassi, in a yellow protective gown, stood nearby, grimacing. "Whoops," she said. "I'll clean it up, I promise. It was a gift I bought for you. Hey, you're awake!"

Water lay amid a broken crystal pitcher on the linoleum floor.

"Gift?" said Merrill, but what came out was a grunt. Merrill noticed to her left the ventilator tube emerging from her mouth that led to a machine with pumping noises. It forced her to breathe, and Merrill hated that sensation. She wanted to breathe by herself, damn it. A clear IV line shot into the crook of her left arm, and wires emerged from under her gown. She was the bionic woman, meat at the end of medical methodology. Instantly she wanted to be back at the waterfalls. There at least she was healthy.

"Dan," she tried to say, but the tube made it sound like another grunt.

"What?" said Stassi moving closer. "You can't really talk with that in your throat." Stassi wore latex gloves. "Should I get a nurse?"

Merrill shook her head and repeated "Dan."

"I'm sorry, I can't understand," Stassi said. "But you're okay! Isn't that great? You made it through the operation."

During the summer, when she couldn't get pregnant and Dan seemed angrier all the time, Merrill had had problems breathing. At first she'd thought it was her asthma or maybe even panic attacks, but a battery of tests gave her the news she had obstructive hypertrophic cardiomyopathy. Trying to overcome the obstructive component, the heart had become overmuscled and stiff, reducing its output and putting backup pressure on her lungs. Her lungs no longer fully oxygenated her blood, so she was very short of breath.

"It's congenital," she'd told her sister one day at Burger King. A clear breathing line had led from Merrill's nose to a portable oxygen tank on wheels at her side. "It's funny—nothing I did—just in the genes."

"Funny?" said Stassi.

"Not funny as in ha-ha," Merrill had said, taking off the nose clip to eat an onion ring right. "Funny as in what timing—a perfect ending to an absurd life."

"It's not an ending. Don't talk that way."

"I can continue breathing one-hundred-percent oxygen until I slowly succumb to suffocation, or I can have open-heart surgery at Mayo and die on the table." The Mayo Clinic was only seventy miles south in Rochester, Minnesota. "They want to stop my heart, cut it open, and slice some inner muscle away in the way we clean out a pumpkin at Halloween."

"What do you mean it's in the genes?" asked Stassi.

"It means you might have it, too."

"Oh, great."

"Get yourself an echocardiogram. It's an easy test. They rub something like KY Jelly on your chest, but instead of having your husband play your hooters like bicycle horns, they skate a device the size of a stapler over you to see your heart."

"Huh?"

"They look at your chambers and valves in motion."

"An ultrasound?"

"Yeah. Like you had for your last baby."

"Might my babies have this disease, too?"

"Maybe."

"Shit." Stassi seemed to ponder that over a few bites of Whopper, then said, "You're going for the surgery, I hope."

"I don't know."

"You're not going to die," said Stassi as a statement.

Merrill had accepted her pronouncement then as well as now. Clearly the surgery had worked. All had gone as planned. Her heart was repaired, sewn back up, restarted, and functioning again. What a strange world this was.

"You're okay," Stassi now said.

Merrill let herself drop back into the bed, and it hurt like falling onto a frozen lake. She closed her eyes.

* * *

She was a brain floating in fog. Merrill felt sad she'd lost her body. She could see the ridges of her brain looking like a topographical map of a desert mountain chain. There was a place that looked perfect for a golf course. She couldn't golf, she realized, but then again, golf looked boring.

Now her eyes flickered open, and a blond-haired nurse in a yellow protective gown pulled up a light blanket closer to Merrill's chin.

"There you are," the woman said. "I'm Kirsten, your day nurse. Would you like the back of your bed raised?" Merrill must have nodded because Kirsten pressed a button on the side of her bed, and Merrill felt her back rise toward a sitting position. Kirsten was a Swedish name. Swedes loved lingonberries.

Merrill could have had her own lingonberry patch if she'd stayed in Sweden, but she chose here. Choices.

Only then did Merrill notice the tube was no longer in her mouth.

"You're probably feeling out of it, huh?" said Kirsten. "Your signs were so good, the doctor lowered your morphine dose, then later took out the ventilator tube. Is your throat sore?"

With shaky hands, Merrill felt her throat. Oh. That was the outside.

Merrill looked down at the break in her hospital gown and saw wires attached to her chest on either side of her medium-sized breasts, breasts that had been adored by top photographers and fashion designers around the world for a good ten years. Her chest now had a huge line down the middle with stitches. Who'd hire her now with a rope-looking scar? Still, she wasn't dead. The open-heart surgery had worked.

"Your aunt and sister are in the waiting room. Should I get them?"

"Anyone else?" Merrill said, her throat now feeling raw and sore.

"Just those two now. You want to see them?"

No. Merrill shook her head and closed her eyes.

* * *

"Honey?" she heard. Aunt Jackie was there with her Pillsbury smile, 350 pounds of love. Aunt Jackie and her husband had taken in Merrill and Stassi as young teenagers when their parents had died in a small-airplane accident. "How do you feel?"

"I feel something." Merrill thought her voice in her dry throat now sounded like a diesel truck smashing into a concrete pylon. "What day is it?"

"Tuesday. Does it matter?"

"Tuesdays have a lot of hope."

Aunt Jackie laughed.

"Any water?" Merrill asked.

"Absolutely," said Aunt Jackie, bringing a clear plastic cup with a straw from the bedside table up to Merrill's mouth. Aunt

Jackie had been a seamstress as they went through high school, and later, as Merrill's modeling career flourished, Merrill had given Aunt Jackie money to open her own fabric store. It proved to be a hit.

Merrill took the cup and found her hand shaking. She drank. "Better," said Merrill. "Is Dan here?"

Surprise crossed Aunt Jackie's face. "No, but I'm sure when he hears the tube is out, he'll come." She took Merrill's hand. "I know you two have been having a hard time. I've always said most husbands are like horseshoes. It's rare you get one spot on, but close counts."

"Same with suicide bombers."

"Now, let's just have positive thoughts, okay?" said her aunt, towering at her side.

Merrill shrugged. She and Dan had been married only two years, but it'd felt longer. Which restaurant to eat at, which movie to see, when to have sex, procreative or otherwise, had all became sources of debate. So why the hell did she want to please him so much? She knew. He'd always seemed so sure of himself—a nice trait. He'd been sure they were soul mates.

She'd been previously engaged to a Swedish baron. The baron was her age and handsome except for a crook in his nose. He'd promised her wealth, the world stage, and his infidelity. That is, he had wanted to maintain his stream of mistresses. He was honest about it, but she didn't want to be first wife in a modern-day harem. Rather, she moved back to Iowa and later met Dan, a Minnesotan who bought and sold grain for Cargill. Trouble began when she couldn't produce a kid.

A flickering caught her attention. The flat-screen TV suspended from the ceiling was on, news muted with closed captioning. Aunt Jackie must have been watching. An image of a container ship was shown floundering, a black shroud around it—oil. There must be a breach in the hull, thousands of gallons of oil spilling into a bay. Merrill realized it was the perfect image of her marriage.

"Can't get pregnant, and now this," said Merrill. "There's no ride like this at Disneyland."

"I suppose you're right," said her aunt.

They were silent. What else was there to say? Merrill cleared her throat. "Did I tell you I read about the history of this place?" she said.

"The Mayo Clinic?"

Merrill nodded. "A lot of famous people have been helped here, including Ernest Hemingway and Art Garfunkel. Wouldn't it have been funny if they'd sung 'Bridge Over Troubled Waters' here together?"

Aunt Jackie nodded as if following Merrill's thoughts. "God knows your uncle's been patient with me."

"My husband isn't like yours."

Aunt Jackie considered, then said, "No, Dan isn't."

"Okay," said Merrill. They left it at that.

"I'm feeling tired," said Merrill to Aunt Jackie, who was arranging the small gifts on her dresser. Flowers weren't allowed on the floor, but small gifts were.

"Someone sent you cookies," said Aunt Jackie. "You rest, and I'll take care of the cookies."

* * *

When Merrill next awoke, Dan was reading *Track and Field* in a chair, sunlight in his close-cropped hair. He looked as handsome as when they'd met at Stassi's wedding. Both in the wedding party, they'd been paired up, he, Best Man, she, Maid of Honor.

"You're here," Merrill now said softly.

"And you're alive," said Dan. "Isn't that great?"

"You weren't here earlier."

"I had a luncheon I couldn't get out of."

"You were at Nichole's house, weren't you?"

He didn't deny it but scooted his chair forward. "I suppose this is as good a time as any. After all, you're into a new chapter of your life."

"I can't even read yet. I can hardly focus."

"I'm talking about us."

"I know."

"What kind of ass would I be if I left while you were sick? But now you're not sick, see? Truth is, I've been an anchor around your neck. This is a gift. You have a whole new life in front of you, and this is really a good time for... you know. "

"You mean de-anchoring. You're setting my neck free?"

"Your career slowdown was bound to change our lives."

"As if I had a choice."

"It was just obvious, wasn't it? A model is only a seasonal kind of thing."

"Right. At thirty-six, my season is now autumn. Before the operation, it was winter. And how old is Nichole? Mid-twenties? And fecund?"

"You don't have to call her names."

"Fecund means she's capable of producing offspring—or fruit or vegetation."

"Thank you, Miss Dictionary."

A nurse came rushing in. She looked at Dan with a frown, then at Merrill. "I saw your heart rate jump up." She looked at the monitor above her bed. "It's coming back down. Conversation sometimes brings anxiety."

"Yeah, sometimes," said Merrill.

"I guess I better go," said Dan.

"Yes. I suppose so."

He stood, glanced at her, then walked out as casually as a man noticing a newsstand.

* * *

Seven months later, a young man and woman, late teens, kicked a soccer ball in an emerald field. Merrill sat inside her car in the SCCAD parking lot next to the field sketching the young man and woman's gestures. Her car, a Dodge Intrepid, was a fifteen-year-old model in a faded red. She'd bought it after she sold her Mercedes, which was paying for the first year of school at the Southern California College of Art and Design—commonly referred to as "Scad." The school had multiple programs in the performing and fine arts. With her divorce still in process, which had left her with little, she needed this new direction. She'd been accepted into the fine arts program.

Before she left Minnesota, she'd met with her cardiologist, who told her she was fine, that her heart was working well and it would, over the next year, remodel. Her car, she realized, was an old model; her heart, a remodel.

Today was the first day of classes, and she'd arrived early. She had time to kill—so she was drawing. She drew to keep her mind occupied more than anything else. After all, the art program focused on conceptual art—she didn't have to draw at all. The program was about ideas. If she hadn't known how to draw, she could hire someone who could. With performance art encouraged, she could even give a performance piece about drawing—in her case, all about the things she couldn't draw: rabbits and anger management and a new life that made her want to throw up.

She also couldn't draw knees well, or a cat's mysterious stare, or the hope she had had on her wedding day at the Unitarian Church where the minister's smile had stretched exactly from pupil to pupil—proportions as perfect as Michelangelo. Merrill, however, could draw losing. It was a mere scratch through a face or a line down the middle of one's chest.

She now stared at the couple kicking the soccer ball, waiting for a perfect moment. There. The girl was about to kick the ball at her boyfriend. They grinned, new lovers, no doubt. Merrill wanted to draw that: optimism, possibility, faith. Merrill gave herself two minutes to draw both figures. The idea was to get the passion on the page through quick, light pencil strokes. Make the pencil follow the intention flashed to the brain. Once you have the shape, use bold lines where gravity pulled. Show where the force was.

Merrill tried to capture their pureness, too. She wished she was better at this. Nonetheless, she described well the girl's open face, suggesting life was fecund. Merrill X'd everything out. This was stupid, the whole art school thing. Just because she'd modeled for an artist and lived with him for five years didn't mean she knew art. Graham Kingman was before the Swedish prince and before Dan. This parking lot was her life after them.

She started a sketch of Dan as she remembered him, determined to get something down in her sketchbook. Surely she'd have to show something today, the first day. Dan she knew. She sculpted the way his skull indented a little more at the eyes than most people. His eyes showed compassion—well, they once did. That's the way she wanted to remember him, not the way he was with the mediator as they divided up the little that was left after the debt. After they'd married, they each had made good money, but she and Dan had always spent quickly—on a house that lost value, and on boats, cars and traveling.

She scratched out Dan and opened her car door, straightening her red dress that covered her scar but showed her figure to good advantage. She placed her small tote with wheels on the ground. She wasn't going to use a backpack as she had in high school—that wouldn't go with the dress. Her clothes were the only things she had left of worth, some of them from the best designers, perks of her work.

She stepped from the car, pulled her bag, and felt real again. The main building was where she had to go, and she told herself to enter as if she owned the place, just like on the runway. Think positively. Walk. Enjoy the stares. Indeed, as she moved up the steps, boys in baggy shorts gazed at her, stopping. Did they recognize her from her magazine covers? No, they were too young. No one remembers, anyway. It showed she dressed right, though.

As she marched toward the set of glass doors, her breath came up short. Was this a problem with her heart? Her anxiety, she realized, coursed as a river through her. She stepped to the shadows of a brick wall. She fiddled with her cell phone as if looking up information. Is this what her life had come to, a faded model faking something?

* * *

Professor Bennett, tall, lanky, with earnest gray hair and blue jeans, strode back and forth in front of the Writing Arts class as Merrill watched self-consciously.

"Writing is thinking," he said. "I teach here because I believe this. Great artwork comes from great thinkers—and great thinkers write."

She hadn't been in a classroom since high school in Davenport, Iowa, and now here she was, seven months beyond her heart operation, near broke, and older than most of the other students. While she had hated high school, she'd always been a voracious reader. When on the road and other models were into drugs, she would read philosophy and novels—Kierkegaard and Anne Rice, Heidegger and Margaret Atwood, Lacan and Barbara Kingsolver, the male and the female. Still, had such reading given her security? Did it help with Dan?

To settle herself now, she tried to imagine what kind of print ad the professor would be in if he weren't pacing and teaching. Something mechanical. Put him in a black cotton shirt, give him a gray-and-yellow bagless vacuum cleaner, and he could sell Dysons.

"Picasso," said the professor, "wrote as prolifically as he painted. From 1936 on, he wrote relentlessly, mostly prose poems. To make the great leaps in art that he did, he had to think. He came to love writing, and he thought he'd be remembered, in fact, as a Spanish poet—someone who'd dabbled in painting, drawing, and sculpture." The instructor laughed. "Sometimes we can't see ourselves, eh?"

The professor strode to the board and wrote, "To write is to think."

Merrill thought about Graham Kingman, whom she'd lived with in New York while she was in her twenties. He'd been obsessive about his journal, often sketching things in there, too. Later, when he'd become famous and moved to California, the University of California Los Angeles bought a bronze version of Merrill, naked, for its sculpture garden. She'd be forever young near the North Campus grill. Kingman ended up marrying a movie star, but he and Merrill had remained friends, and he'd written a great recommendation for her SCCAD application. Writing worked.

Professor Bennett stopped and faced the class head-on. "I want to see how you think. I want to learn a little bit about each of you, too, so the first thing I want you to do is write about a day in your life where something changed. This is a real event. I want to see that you have moments, memories that are important. It'll give me a clue to how you see things."

Next to her, a tall young man with an angular face leaned toward her. His hands were the size of ballet dancers. "Might you have an extra pencil or pen and some paper?" he said. As Merrill looked around, she noticed many other students in the classroom asking others for the same thing. How could anyone go to a writing class without paper and a pen? Did they think success came from osmosis?

"Yeah, sure," she said and looked in her wheeled pack. She gave him a fresh spiral notebook and a steel-pointed pen. He reminded her of a Rodin statue.

"I just need a couple pages," he said, ripping out two sheets and handing her back the book.

"You might need it for the semester," she said. She had noticed him earlier glancing her way often. He was too young for her, but she was glad for the interest. Still, she didn't need any men in her life right now.

"My loan should be coming through any day. I just need two sheets for now." He handed back the notebook. "My name's Eli O'Rourke," he said. "Can I take you out for coffee afterwards to thank you?"

"Without your loan?"

"I mean I—"

"That's okay," she said, shaking her head.

"Just a quick coffee?"

"I'm still moving in. I've a lot to do."

"Okay. Thanks for the paper and pen, though."

"No problem."

"The main thing," said the professor, "is I want you to grasp that writing is like any other art. You build in layers. Just write quickly. Improve it later. Genius will slip in this way."

Merrill raised her hand. The professor smiled, his eyes shuttling between her face and her chest. "Yes?" he said.

"Are we writing a creative piece or just information?"

"It's a memory—a day that changed you. You must have a moment that says something to you."

"Many."

"Good," he said. "Write about one. Twenty minutes."

She set to work and wrote without worry. *"You're going to die,"* the doctor said, *"unless you have an operation." I sat in the small examination room and looked at his wall. There was a giant poster of a heart, labeled with the parts. Right atrium, left ventricle, tricuspid valve, and more. I had all these things, but I also had too much. Too much heart. I would need part of my heart muscle cut out.*

The doctor wore round wire-rim glasses like John Lennon, but this man was in his fifties and had visible pores on his face. His hair was gray. Perhaps this is what Lennon would have looked like if he'd not been shot four times in the back at the age of forty. One bullet had cut Lennon's aorta, and he died from blood loss. Might I be joining Lennon, soon? Imagine.

She continued to write quickly, contrasting her heart beating at the Mayo Clinic to Dan's heart beating next to Nichole's—she, a waitress he'd met at the Original Pancake House not far from their large lakeside home. *How blind I'd been, then. I knew nothing of Nichole, did not smell her scent on his body. Then again, noticing scents was a luxury I no longer had. With my breathing labored, Dan and I had stopped making love, stopped even the daily affection of holding each in the bed in morning.*

Before I'd married, I'd worked steadily for Victoria's Secret, made it to the Sports Illustrated *swimsuit issue twice, and had choice gigs in Europe. You don't have to live in New York or Paris to model once you make it. But now I couldn't model with an oxygen tank at my side. And Dan was adding his syrup to the pancake lady. I was betrayed—by my body and by my husband.*

She paused and thought about where she was now. The fact was, this was her new life. If she did poorly at school, she knew she'd spiral down into the kind of despair from which she might not emerge.

So many of my moments were low, I can't rate the worst. Was it when I'd been in ICU for three weeks post-surgery and post-Dan? I'd begged Aunt Jackie and Stassi to let me die. In that bed, I'd quickly lost muscle tone and could barely move my arms and legs at one point. My doctor prescribed anti-anxiety medication and, for depression, Celexa, both of which I still use. A week of physical therapy, then rejoining my gym and trainer daily brought my muscle tone back. But am I really back?

After twenty minutes, Professor Bennett said, "Please stop." A few people shook their wrists as if they weren't used to using a pen.

"Who'd like to read his or her piece aloud?" asked the professor. No one raised a hand. The professor looked around. When his gaze came to Merrill, she meekly hoisted a few fingers.

"You'll read?"

She nodded.

"Wonderful," he said. "Could you stand so people in the back can hear you?"

She nodded. Merrill spoke her written words, and the few times she looked up from the pages, she saw people were nodding, deeply interested. She skipped the part about her being a model. She didn't want people to know her as that. She was just a girl from Minnesota who had a heart operation and became divorced. "As I was learning to use a walker after two weeks in ICU—my muscles had atrophied that quickly—I could only guess that Dan was eating pancakes with Nichole. He filed for divorce on my last day on the rehab floor. I don't quite understand this life. I knew about this art school, though. It was far away. That's where I wanted to be. I am here. I need to find my new life."

People clapped, including the professor. "Excellent," he said. "At times like this, I see myself not so much an instructor but as an art director. Well done."

Other people read their pieces. One woman wrote about her rape at gunpoint. A bearded young man told of spending a night at his friend's house when he was fourteen and taking a lot of acid without telling anyone. His friend's father showed them *Full Metal Jacket,* a film about Vietnam. He spent the night shaking in his sleeping bag, hallucinating, feeling he was the sniper and swearing he'd be dead by the morning. Eli spoke about his tree house, which he'd loved until he witnessed someone being shot in the alley visible from his tree. He was eleven years old at the time and gave evidence that led to a teenager's arrest. Merrill shook her head—too many guns. She also realized people were just beer cans: we're all crushed by something.

"How old are you now?" someone asked Eli.

"Thirty," he said.

Merrill looked at him anew. Thirty?

When the class ended and she was walking out, she noticed Eli approach her. He was about to say something when the professor said, "Merrill—may I speak with you a moment?" Eli then just nodded to Merrill and continued on.

The professor was at his desk packing his book bag. "Thank you for reading today," he said as she stepped up. "It broke the ice in the class."

"Thank you."

"Do you have a moment for a coffee? There's a coffee nook here if you haven't discovered it."

"Yes, sure," she said, then looked at the door. Eli stood there. He shook his head and left. She winced. She never liked hurting anyone.

The coffee nook was down the wide, windowless hallway. She pulled her pack along. For an art college on top of a gorgeous hill, she'd been surprised at the lack of windows. The Mayo Clinic hospital she'd been in had been less sterile than this white-walled place. Still, what counted were the people inside, and she prided herself she'd already made an impression with one of her professors.

They turned into an open door framed by glass bricks. "Have a seat," said the professor as they entered, indicating a set of round stainless steel tables with chairs. The room blessedly was awash in windows opening out to where bright red bougainvillea bloomed. In the distance, brown desert hills like leftover dinner buns framed a valley of tract homes and eucalyptus tress. "Cappuccino?" he asked.

"Thanks." She reached for her money in her rolling pack when he said, "No, my treat."

"Thank you." She had the awful feeling he was hitting on her. Wasn't there a rule professors couldn't? Or was she being naïve? She nodded to herself. She still had the capacity to be naïve—good. Perhaps there was hope for her.

Professor Bennett paid the young woman at the coffee bar, and he returned with two large paper cups of foamy drink.

"Thanks," she said taking one. "Are you sure you don't want money?"

"It's nothing. I wanted to find out more about you."

"Oh?"

"Your lovely piece didn't mention your modeling."

"So you know."

"I've been a *Sports Illustrated* subscriber for years. I remember you in there. You were great."

"I'm older now," she said. "And as you saw in my writing, I need a new direction."

"Why this? Americans don't particularly want artists."

"What do you mean?"

"As opposed to your running a modeling agency or making a reality show or, what—marrying a rich guy?"

"Isn't that cynical?"

He laughed. "I suppose. Sorry. Sometimes I'm worse and ask what's the point of anything? We're just aimlessly toddling on until our clocks run out."

She nodded. "We're just 'beings toward death,' right? Martin Heidegger said we're all looking for an authentic life before the inevitable happens. We're supposed to face death and have a healthy anxiety towards it."

He smiled. "I'm impressed." He sipped his drink and grimaced. "Hot."

"With my operation and then my divorce, what's left? Maybe it's art. I'm hoping it's art."

"The best students—which clearly you'll be—slam ideas together, and it gets people thinking. That's what artists should do. But this place can have a lot of jealousy and competition, especially during crits. You have to ask yourself if this is what you need. I mean if Heidegger were here, he'd find, yes, one has to confront death but one also has to confront crits." He laughed.

"It's this or nothing," she said.

"Even if people pick everything you do apart?"

"Same happens in modeling."

He laughed again. "I bet you're right. It's blood sport." He lifted his coffee in a toast. "Then you're in the right place."

At that moment, Eli entered, carrying his backpack. When she noticed him, he glowered, but she smiled at him and shrugged her shoulders. He nodded and stepped up to the coffee bar, his back to them.

Professor Bennett noticed. "Do you want to invite him over?"

"No. I just met him today. I'm not looking for a date."

He grinned widely. "I hope you don't mistake my advice or your coffee," he said. "I'm extremely lucky with the woman I live with—another professor here, actually. Between her, my son, my ex-wife, and— Well, more than you want to know, but I'm about as happy as a man like me can be. I just give advice."

"No, I wasn't thinking you—"

"My advice is to be careful here."

* * *

Merrill sat in a chair in the Green Gallery, one of four student galleries at SCAAD. The room wasn't the color green but was named after a donor, Justice Green, an alumnus of the art program who went on to do well in the New York art scene in the seventies—before the art scene had been scooped up by Los Angeles. Her painting workshop instructor, Mr. Bezos, a well-known artist who had stopped painting to write art criticism, sat in an identical blue plastic chair as did the remaining eleven members of her painting workshop class. They faced the wall and Merrill's 16 x 20 painting called "Ellen Before the Fall." A muscular runway model with long blond hair wore only a purple two-piece swimsuit. She was taking an overly long step and looked like she was slipping.

"Really, come on," said Sandra, a second-year student, twenty years old. Sandra licked the stud in her lip. "Do we really need this iconography? A model, for Christ's sake?"

"Yeah," said Dobbs, a chubby young man who loved to paint action scenes of dog fights. "Don't we get enough of this shit on the magazine covers at the grocery store?"

"Derivative," said a young woman behind her.

"Derivative of whom?" said Mr. Bezos.

"Helmut Newton, the photographer?" said the voice.

"Exactly so," said Mr. Bezos, grabbing the lapels of his sports coat over his black t-shirt. "As you all probably know, Helmet Newton was a fashion photographer who liked large busty women, but he was also a master of telling a story in a small space. What other strengths did Newton have as a photographer?"

"None," said Sandra. "He exploited women for commercial gain."

"Yes," said the woman next to Merrill with pink hair who seemed to have been seething up until now. "Everything Merrill has shown this semester has been splashy, commercial shit. Completely derivative."

Merrill turned to Mr. Bezos. "And we're not supposed to allude to others ever or be adept in our work because, God forbid, someone might want to buy it? I'm not thrilled with—"

"Are you supposed to be thrilled?" said Dobbs.

Merrill shook her head. If they don't get what she's after, then what's the point? What else could she do? She felt as if she were whirling down a drain.

"Look at your subject matter," said Mr. Bezos to Merrill. His cool smile betrayed an edge of disappointment. "How can we not help but think of Newton?"

"Helmut Newton was inventive as a fashion photographer," Merrill said. "I came to know him."

"Is that supposed to impress us?" said Sandra.

"I don't care what—"

"Merrill, please," said Mr. Bezos. "Hold off your thoughts until the others are finished."

"Like I'm carrion?" said Merrill.

"Isn't your subject a piece of meat?" said the pink-haired girl.

Silence descended like a scythe. Everyone sat there and continued to stare. Merrill sighed. She'd really expected more from these critiques, but no matter who was being critiqued, the same handful of people always found negative things to say, and most of the others seemed either too shallow or too afraid to say things beyond "It's interesting," "Good use of color," or "There's a lot of potential here." Mr. Bezos tended to point out what was iconic, symbolic, and indexical.

"What you're all saying just makes me laugh," came a male voice from the back. "It's like you're looking but you can't see."

Merrill turned, surprised. Eli O'Rourke smiled. He'd always been one of the quiet ones, and while he'd been cordial to Merrill in class, now three months in, they really had not conversed.

"What do you see, Mr. O'Rourke?" said the instructor.

"First all all, hasn't anyone noticed what's on the woman's swimsuit?" People moved forward in their seats to look more carefully.

"Rhinoceroses," said Eli. "Is that just random, or do we consider that Merrill is offering symbolism here?"

"Galloping penises?" said another of the quiet ones, an international student from Korea, a tall young man with black glasses.

Merrill smiled. Okay. Now they're looking.

"I think so," said Eli. "If we assume this is a fashion model, then the subject's world is about galloping penises. And she's falling—her action, right? So it's not as if the model is in complete control. Helmut Newton's women were always in control, brazen, you might say, but this one, falling, is about as vulnerable as you can be. So would you say she's in control?"

"I see," said the Korean guy.

"Frankly," said Eli, "you're all not looking deeply because why? You assume that because Merrill was a former model means she's not as intelligent as you are? I think she just bested you."

Mr. Bezos nodded, then smiled. "That may be true," he said. "If we saw this in a gallery and didn't know the artist, we might be looking at it another way."

"Isn't this painting showing us what we're like as artists?" said Eli. "Vulnerable and open to attack?"

"Or blessed with beauty and things will always be okay?" said Sandra.

"Try aging," said Merrill.

Sandra, Dobbs, and the pink-haired girl remained mute and sullen, still not ready to buy into the conclusion. Merrill realized that she, too, hadn't been looking clearly enough at Eli until now. She nodded her thanks, and he nodded back.

* * *

Thursday night at SCAAD brought art openings. Two hours into her show, Merrill refilled bowls with peanuts and M&Ms, moving about in her black high-neck Dolce and Gabbana dress with its silver metallic detailing.

"Good show," said Professor Bennett, pointing in particular to "Ellen Before the Fall."

"Nice dress," said his girlfriend, Professor Wilson.

"Thank you both for coming. This means the world to me," said Merrill.

Wearing black jeans and a SCCAD t-shirt, Eli helped Merrill refill the bowls for chips and guacamole, and the Korean young man, Zesung, approved by the Office of Student Affairs to serve alcohol to people with the over-21 wrist bands, poured wine. The three of them weren't drinking but keeping everyone happy. As with the other openings, the student whose work was being displayed paid for and hosted his or her party. For Merrill, this was a financial sacrifice, but she wanted to do it right—plenty of food and drink for all—a few hundred people so far.

Just after one a.m., the wine ran out, and soon so did the people. "I can't thank you enough, Eli," said Merrill. "I'm sorry I didn't get to know you earlier."

"De nada."

"I was going to suggest sharing some wine, but there's nothing left."

"I've got beer," he said.

"Where?" she said.

"My dorm."

"Oh. You live there?"

"It's not so bad."

"It's not so bad!" shouted Zesung, gathering the wine bottles into a giant blue plastic recycle bin. He handed her a remaining half bottle of red. "I've saved you two a bottle. You two share. I'll finish cleaning."

"Really?" said Merrill. Zesung nodded, apparently happy to have helped.

"To the dorm!" she said.

They giggled on the way over, stopping first under a tree to share the wine. Merrill realized she hadn't felt this free and happy since long before she learned of her heart condition. They held each other as they strolled to the dorm.

When they moved down the dorm's beige cinder-block hallway, each room number cheaply stenciled on white doors, she smelled marijuana and heard sound systems compete with each other. Rap music boomed on one side, hard metal on another. She felt uneasy. This wasn't her generation.

Eli unlocked his door and flipped on the lights. His single bed stood against a wall with skateboard posters, and empty Guinness beer cans were strewn about like dead crows. He was thirty years old? The moment sobered her. What was she doing here?

"Have a roommate?" she asked.

"Nope."

She nodded and pulled back one of the curtains. Below, a young couple hugged on the concrete at the edge of a blue-lit swimming pool. They appeared to be naked, and they took a step and fell toward the water, breaking its surface and plunging in. They parted, laughing.

"Nice view of the pool," said Merrill.

"See, the dorms aren't so bad."

"I'd better go," she said.

"But I thought we were—"

"You've been an absolute gentleman," she assured him. I just—"

"Come on, we're artists."

That caught her. *Artist.* If you called yourself something, maybe you could be it. "Yes, but—"

"I don't want to be a gentleman," he added and held his arms out. The look on his face was so damn certain, as sure as Dan had always been. She moved into his arms, and he kissed her. He tasted like merlot. He had an intensity she loved, as if his lips were made from the original hydrogen of the sun. This was the place to be. She and he were artists.

She worked at his belt, and after his pants slid down, she pulled down his briefs. She stood back and stared. He clearly worked out, yet with one hand on her shoulder, he looked innocent. The guy had an amazing gene pool. Perfection.

"Were your parents both models?" she asked.

He frowned. "Mom's a lawyer. Dad has a marketing firm." Eli stepped up to her and unzipped her dress, which slithered down. She wore no bra, just a thong. He stared like the first child to find a TV. She realized: her scar. Damn. She covered herself with her arms.

"I'm sorry, I'm sorry," and she reached down for her dress.

"No, what? You're beautiful."

"Not with this—"

"That's the coolest scarification I've ever seen. Are you pierced anywhere, too?"

"This?" She touched the twisted scar under her thumb.

"Can I?" and he reached out and fingered its length. It tickled. "Did you get this done in L.A.?"

"It's from heart surgery."

"Oh, that's right." He covered her breast with his large hand over her heart. "Wow."

And she kissed him. She'd never kissed anyone so handsome. The others weren't ugly by any means, but this guy, exceptional, so helpful, so hopeful.

She imagined her heart waves as she'd once seen on the monitor next to her bed. A cursor dove down a green stream and blipped in earthquake coughs regularly.

Her arms and legs now wrapped around Eli, and he walked to his single bed, cascading them down like geese to a river past the cattails. The bed then squeaked, but in the moment he entered her, his wonderful galloping penis, the same squeak sang out. They were artists. Artists. Artists. Art. Mozart.

* * *

"Breathe steadily, come on," said Aunt Jackie, dressed in a yellow protective gown. "Don't lose your energy."

"I have plenty of energy," said Merrill, "but it feels like... I don't know."

"Don't push," said Stassi. "Be calm."

"Like I'm taking a dump. I feel wet," said Merrill.

They were at the Mayo. Merrill liked the Mayo, trusted the Mayo. And her cervix was at four centimeters.

With her laxtex-gloved hand, Stassi lifted the sheet. "Yep, your water finally broke. Maybe I should tell the nurse."

"Wait a moment," said Merrill. She glanced to the monitors. His heartbeat was steady at 145. Hers was 80. They were a heartbeat samba. "Help me with the Lamaze thing."

"Right. Relax," said Stassi, taking her hand. "Remember: think of a calm place, a great place."

Merrill thought of Eli's bedroom that night. That was the best place of her life.

"Have you changed your mind?" asked Aunt Jackie. "Should we call the baby's father?"

Merrill cringed at the pain in her lower back, then burst out laughing.

"What?" said Stassi.

"The baby's father, Eli," said Merrill, "is only nineteen. He told me thirty."

"What?" said Stassi. "You couldn't see?"

Merrill shook her head. The contractions stopped, and she sighed in relief.

"Why couldn't you tell us about him before?" said Aunt Jackie.

"You mean besides my feeling like I'm being tortured right now?"

"Yeah."

"It's complicated." She controlled her breath again. "He doesn't want the information out."

"Like we'll tell anyone?" said Stassi.

"Eli's mother called me shortly after we found out—she's a lawyer. She wanted me to terminate, said her son wasn't ready to be a father. I said he should have thought of that when he didn't use protection. Of course, I didn't think I needed any. You know—with Dan."

"Maybe Dan was shooting blanks," offered Aunt Jackie. "Ever get tested?"

"No. But I told his Mom this might be my only chance, what with my past history and my time clock running out. She said her son couldn't afford a child."

"And he didn't want to be here?" said Stassi.

Merrill remembered walking down the hallway, dressed in jeans, trying to remember his room number. She found it. He was surprised to see her. She'd told him weeks earlier that she wasn't ready for another relationship. It was too soon. She then showed him the positive blue plus on the indicator, and he started crying. As he was crying, she was thinking how he had such beautiful DNA. They'd have a gorgeous baby. And his swimmers must have been aggressive. This was meant to be. "He was having a hard time. I feel bad about that."

She felt another contraction starting. "He wasn't happy... I said he... he didn't need to be a Dad... I just wanted to be a Mom." The contraction hit hard but she resisted pushing.

Stassi moved to the foot of the bed and started to massage Merrill's feet. "What'd you say to his mom?"

Merrill at that moment felt absolutely energized. She didn't expect this. "I told her don't worry. She asked was I willing to sign a form to take full responsibility? I said. 'Give me hospital costs, we'll call it even, and I'll sign.' So I signed."

"Still, I worry about the money," said Aunt Jackie. "Do you want to work in the shop?"

"I told you I got a scholarship," said Merrill, who then screamed at a sudden pain. "The baby's coming!"

"It's too early. Sorry to say, but it usually takes hours with drama and emotion," said Aunt Jackie calmly while lifting the sheet.

"It's been only forty-five minutes," said Stassi.

"Babies don't—" Aunt Jackie gasped. "I'll get the doctor. The baby's coming!" The sound of Aunt Jackie's heavy corduroy pants zipped out the door in concert with the staccato punctuation of her clogs. She sounded like a hollow birch tree running away.

Soon a green-gowned nurse rushed in. She was African-American and older than Merrill. "Don't push, don't push." The nurse transferred Merrill to a wheel chair.

"He's coming, he's coming," said Merrill to the nurse. "So will I have stretch marks forever?"

"Stretch marks will be the least of your worries, honey."

They quickly glided down the corridor, and Merrill imagined she was skiing, which she'd learned in Switzerland. The speed was fun, the clothes, great. They now shushed into a birthing room. Dr. Judy Feinberg and another nurse helped Merrill into the reclining bed, as a heavily breathing Aunt Jackie watched.

"Are you okay?" asked Merrill of her aunt.

"Of course I am. The diet starts next week."

Stassi pulled out her camera and started taking photos. Merrill spread her legs, eager as a tuning fork. "He's coming."

"The head!" said Aunt Jackie, "He has hair, dark hair."

"I've got it," said Stassi, clicking away.

The little fellow slipped right out—like a child on a waterslide. "It's a boy all right," said the doctor. The baby started crying.

"Ah," said Merrill in relief. And she couldn't help herself, her whole body convulsed in happiness and tears.

A nurse took the boy and weighed him on a scale. "Seven pounds, two ounces."

In a few more minutes, the placenta came out, and that was weighed. Everything was happening as it was supposed to—like the way dogs had to bark and the best bagels had to have raisins. The doctor was now sewing. Merrill had had the episiotomy after all.

Her boy was handed to her, swaddled in a light flannel blanket with bears. Aunt Jackie and Stassi and the staff were mere blurs in the background. Merrill had not decided on a boy's name, and the many she'd considered rushed at her— Jason, Johnny, Jerold—no, no J names—how about Z? Zebidiah? Her boy was so pink, and his mouth was moving as if he was already talking. She could feel his heart as it drummed with life.

With her index finger, she touched his little muskrat hand, and he grasped her finger. Her heart beneath the fading scar leapt. She knew this was where she was supposed to be. This was authentic. Not conceptual but real—a true work of art. And that was what she would name him: Art.

She laid Art over the scar, over her heart.

Bonus Track: "The Hand"

Much as some musicians add an extra unofficial track to their CDs, and some authors give the first chapter of their next book, I thought I'd do something similar. I happen to be working on a collection of related short stories that all have the same protagonist, Edward, and the book covers nearly thirty years of his life. I was inspired by Melissa Bank's fabulous novel-in-stories, *The Girl's Guide to Hunting and Fishing.*

Thus I'm writing *The Brightest Moon of the Century,* in which Edward, a young Minnesotan, is blessed with an abundance of "experience"—first when his mother dies and next when his father, an encyclopedia salesman, shoehorns Edward into a private boys school where he's tortured and groomed.

All he wants is a girlfriend. Edward stumbles into romance in high school, careens through dorm life in college, and whirls into a tornado of love problems as a mini-mart owner in a trailer park in Alabama and beyond. "The Hand" is the first chapter of that book. See what you think.

"The Hand"

(An Excerpt from *The Brightest Moon of the Century*)

(1968-69)

Near mid-century when Edward was born, the full moon was years from being the brightest. That would happen—in terms of luminosity and size—in the last month of the century. As a child growing up, however, Edward found much splendor and mystery in the moon. It kept changing and following him around, a rock with its own rhythms much like women, and he knew he was years away from understanding them.

When he was in eighth grade, after his mother was gone, Edward felt he'd finally done something right. His father, Stanley, stood at the kitchen sink reading one of Edward's English papers. Edward smiled, waiting for his father to see the letter grade of "A" at the end.

"What's this quote?" said his father, who then read the quoted line aloud. "'The moon on the river looked like a dented hubcap floating on a cesspool. I hated rivers, and my grandfather, Elihu Twain, hated them, too.' You say this is from Mark Twain. Where'd you find this quote?" The man frowned.

"I don't know," Edward said. He had to pause his breakfast spoon in mid-flight, knowing his cornflakes, bathing in the bowl's milk, were about to turn into corn mush. "The encyclo-pedia?"

"Don't you know that there were no hubcaps in those days? And Mark Twain's real name was Samuel Clemens, so his grandfather would be named Clemens, for crissakes, not Twain. And Mark Twain, for your information, had been a steamboat pilot, and he loved rivers—compared them to pearls and opals! Where did you get this quote?"

"I was running out of time, so I had to— I mean—"

"You made it up, didn't you?"

"It was due," Edward said. "And I still got an 'A'."

"I didn't raise you to be a cheater."

"She mostly just wanted to see that we can write an essay, and—"

"It's not even that great of an essay," said his father.

"You're always harping on grades so—"

"Don't you blame this on me."

"It's a good grade. What're we arguing about?" Edward stood, turning to the sink with his bowl.

"And what kind of English teacher couldn't catch such a thing?"

"I don't know."

"Education is the asphalt for the road of life."

"What? Asphalt?"

"The point is next fall you're not going to that waste dump of a school."

"Because of one lousy high-graded paper? Come on!" Edward dumped his now-soggy cereal down the garbage disposal.

His father shook his head. "I've been thinking about this awhile. I want you to have more opportunity than I had. You don't want to be an encyclopedia salesman, do you? I want you to go to McCory."

"But I love where I'm at! It's good asphalt."

The fact was Edward did not love his school, but no one bothered him there. At Eastbrook Junior High School, Edward Meopian was not a wallflower but more like a hearty impercep-tible weed. The girls looked through him, the guys he passed in the hallway nodded once in a while, and the teachers didn't find him distracted or daydreaming so did not pounce on him. He was not someone who was teased—for he wasn't nerdy or outwardly vulnerable. Rather, he came across to most people, certainly to himself, as something of an ottoman or sofa: existing and acceptable. His grades were just above average—not good enough for the jocks to ask him if it was okay to copy his homework. If he were to become a mass murderer down the road, no one would know him well enough to tell the blond TV interviewer, "Yeah, I knew him in junior high, and he was so friendly. Who knew he could turn people's pelvis bones into ash trays."

Rather, he was "Edward Who?"

On Saturday morning two weeks later, his father drove Edward to the McCory School to take the entrance exam. The high-class private school for boys was in a bleak brick structure above the train yards of Minneapolis, Minnesota.

His father said, while dropping Edward off, "Do well on the test or else." Or else what? Would his father force him to go to the public high school where Edward wanted to go anyway? Or would his father allow no friends over for a month? Edward had no friends. What do you take away when you have nothing?

Edward nodded and exited the car. Inside the school in dim hallway, a thin man with a nicotine face led him to a small paneled room where a test waited for him on a wooden desk. Edward sighed, flipped the test open, and did as well as he could on the entrance exam, math and English, because he did not want to be thought of as stupid. At the end of the test was the question, "Why do you want to attend McCory School?" He wrote, "I don't want to. My dad wants me to go." To the question, "What appeals to you about McCory?" he penned, "Nothing. I want to go to a school with girls. There are no girls here."

A week later at breakfast, his father said, "I got a call yesterday."

What was that supposed to mean? His father looked serious.

"From Aunt Barbara?" he tried.

"McCory." He broke out in a grin. "You made it in."

"But I don't want to go to McCory. How can you afford McCory?"

"That's my problem."

"I promise to do better at Eastbrook."

"It's McCory. We'll go shopping for suits soon."

"Suits?"

"You have to wear coats and ties there."

Edward gasped.

"Don't give me that look," said his father. "You're going to be a businessman someday, so you may as well get used to coats and ties now."

"What if I want to be a welder?"

"Then you'll be a gentleman welder. Oh, and one other thing. Because of what you wrote at the end of your test about not wanting to go—they felt you had a maturity issue. You'll be starting in the eighth grade."

"But I passed the eighth grade!" said Edward.

"You shouldn't have written what you did." His father finished his coffee and put his cup in the sink. He beamed at Edward. "You're going to be a McCory boy. Someday you'll thank me."

* * *

As the summer ended, his father took him to the Foursome, a men's store across the bay in Wayzata. With stern looks that demanded silence from Edward, Dad bought him one blue blazer and one pin-stripped double-breasted suit, as if Edward were a thin, gawky banker. His father had never spent such money on him before. His father asked him one question: "Do you know how to tie a tie?" Edward shook his head, wondering how his father expected such a thing. They never went anyplace that demanded a tie, so how was he supposed to have learned? By the same method he had learned about girls, in line at gym?

"I know just the trick for you," said his father, and stepped away. Edward would have followed, but he noticed a college-age woman, very pretty in a flowered dress, adjusting the tie of her smiling, husky boyfriend in what must be a new blue suit.

There was something about her touch, sure and casual, that made Edward stare. As she gazed at her man up and down, the way his mother had once looked at him and his father, Edward wondered if he would ever share such a moment with someone again. Would he ever get a girlfriend?

"Here you go," said his father, carrying two pre-tied ties. "These are called clip-ons. You're slow enough in the morning as it is, so this should help you." His father clipped it on just under Edward's throat as easily as a horse was attached to a tether.

Weeks later, walking stiffly in his blue blazer and clip-on, Edward walked the half mile to the corner where the McCory bus would pick him up. The bus was orange like other school buses, but when he stepped on, only boys in coats and ties stared at him, looking like miniature bank tellers.

"Who are you?" said the first kid, about fourth grade with eyes resembling a gerbil.

"Edward."

"Oh," said the kid. "Got gum?"

"No."

A half hour later, the bus pulled into a long, tree-shrouded drive that took them up the hill to the school. The three-story building called the Upper School technically had no grade levels, but rather "forms," as in English schools. Seniors were Form Six, Juniors, Form Five, etc. Edward was in Form Two, the youngest in the Upper School. The Lower School, a smaller, one-story building a long block away, held grades 3 through 6 as well as Form One. The athletic fields lay between. The three wings of the Upper School formed a U that backed its open end against a berm, giving the central, grassy area in back the feel of a prison yard.

The rooms inside, most of them built for fifteen or fewer students, were small, with chipped blackboards and wood floors that had nearly seventy years of yellowed varnish, the color of dead men's fingernails. The rooms echoed the confinement that Edward soon felt. In between classes, the olive green cement stairs that led to each floor flowed with students, the only time that Edward experienced, in his first days, any sense of positive energy, mainly because each step was that much closer to the final bell. The school motto, "Far from noise and smoke," which was perhaps meant to suggest healthy isolation and the flowering of minds in a quiet, smogless atmosphere, did not take into consideration the horn blasts and diesel exhaust from passing trains below. As Edward would learn, the world was an ironic place.

Within the first week, one of Edward's new classmates, John De Bernieres, a husky kid from his English class who walked as if he had a cigar up his butt, beelined right up to him. "What's your dad do?"

"Why?" said Edward.

"My dad runs a big law firm," said De Bernieres, "Maybe he knows your dad."

"Mine's in publishing." That was a stretch. His father sold encyclopedias.

"Oh." De Bernieres yanked Edward's tie, and when it pulled off, he shouted to no one visible, "Hey, you're right. The new kid has a clip-on!" Word spread quickly. In the olive drab hallways of McCory, his tie was being yanked off dozens of times daily by an equal number of classmates, including Lee Boatswain, son of the president of Northwest Banks, Robert B. Dalton, whose parents later named a large bookstore chain after him, and Reese Freely, son of the CEO of Dairy Queen.

On Sunday night after his first week of McCory, in bed early, Edward wondered what to do about the ties. His stomach felt as if it were a washrag wrung and twisted so hard, soon there would be no more liquid. Maybe his whole body would dry up and disappear.

Staring up into the darkness beyond the deepest moonless night, Edward realized maybe his father wasn't the best person to get him through things. His father no longer understood what it was to be a kid. Edward was simply a responsibility. Edward then thought of the time their Sunday dinners had had three placemats, not two. He remembered how he could be with his mother alone, and with a quick hug and a laugh at something Edward said, the world was made right. Maybe she was a ghost, and he could find her. He really wanted to find her. But even if she came to him now, could she help him with a tie? No. The sense of aloneness overwhelmed him. Edward would have to learn how to tie a tie on his own. But how?

Minutes later, he knocked on his father's bedroom door. Edward was scared to knock on the door, of course, but he had nowhere else to turn, even if his stomach told him not to. "What is it?" barked his father.

"Can I come in?"

"*May* I come in?"

"May I?"

"Yes."

He found his father in bed, the same king-size bed he had shared with Edward's mother, whose last paperback book, Jacqueline Suzanne's *Valley of the Dolls,* was still splayed face down on the bedside table as if she would return. His father looked up from a history book about Rommel.

"Aren't you supposed to be in bed? This is my time. I'm tired," said his father.

"I'm sorry. I just— I was— I mean—"

"Spit it out!"

"A tie. I'd like a regular tie, if that's okay. For school."

"I got you two, didn't I?"

"They're clip-ons, not regular."

"Clip-ons look just fine."

"Not really."

"But they're fast to attach."

"The other kids tie regular ones fast. So will I."

He thought his dad might raise his voice at the possibly impertinent answer, but instead his father said, "You can tie ties now?"

"Yeah... I mean yes." He had entered the room also meaning to ask him how, but now, seeing how irritated his father might be, thought it better to pretend.

"Open my second closet and take any two you want," said his father.

Edward nodded. He opened the closet and, from about fifty ties hanging neatly from their own little bars, looked at all the variations on stripes. Nothing stood out, nothing seemed special, so Edward took one in blue and another in green.

"Thanks," said Edward, and, to his surprise, his father smiled.

On Monday morning, Edward awoke early. He stood in front of the bathroom mirror, the green tie around his neck, determined to be a laughingstock no more. He had seen several people tie ties over the past week; they did so fairly unconsciously on the way to chapel, which is how the day started, in pews listening to the headmaster blather non-denominational stuff about God as a mouse, God as a mountain climber and, lo, God as the great headmaster in the sky. Jowly like former Minnesota senator and U.S. vice president Hubert H. Humphrey, the headmaster also spoke about success through self-discipline and through keeping your hair short—no hair over collars at McCory.

Tie tying, Edward had observed, started with the tie around the neck, so that the thin part and the fat part stood side-by-side on one's chest like Olive Oyl and Bluto. The fat part was supposed to hang down farther than the thin part. Then, in a flurry of crossing and flipping, a knot was made. This was done always so fast, Edward couldn't follow what happened, so now, in front of the mirror, he experimented. He came up with knots, but only things that Boy Scouts might be proud of. None of them would slip to allow him to move the knot toward his neck.

Five knots later, he was no closer to solving the problem, and he could feel tears start to form. Damn it! No tears! He was too old for this stuff. God damn McCory boys. He should just tell his father he hated the place and demand to go back to public school, which had not yet started. No one would know of his week's adventure at McCory—they'd just walk past him in the hall as they always did, and everything would be normal. But his father could get very upset if Edward tried to demand anything. One time his father had become agitated when Edward had asked for eggs scrambled the way his mother had made them—with bigger chunks. His father grabbed Edward by the collar and jammed his face nearly into Edward's, and screamed, "I did not choose this life! I did not choose to be single again, and I did not choose to be a father right away, if you want to know! You better be fucking walking on egg shells if you don't want your butt kicked galley west until Sunday." That was a popular phrase of his father's, "kicked galley west until Sunday." Why not Monday or Wednesday or galley east? And what does direction have to do with a galley? All Edward knew then and now was that he would not be able to get his way.

Edward turned to two pictures of his mother he kept by the sink so that he'd see her first thing each day. He noticed water marks on the glass of one, and he wiped them off. The picture was of his mother when she was a girl, standing on a dock on Lake Minnetonka, braids in her hair, looking hesitatingly at her father, the photographer, who had been known to be as stern as Edward's father. In this picture, his mother was about twelve years old, wearing the kind of dress Dorothy wore in Kansas before the tornado took her to Oz. His mother didn't know then that she'd have a son named Edward, nor that she would die twenty-one years later by slipping on the stairway to the basement carrying a load of dirty laundry. She had hit her head on the stairs, but she didn't die there, nor at the office of Dr. Greene, who had said she had a bump on her head and nothing more, but she died in bed later that night in her sleep. The next morning, when Dad was already at work, Edward was late for his swimming lesson, and Mom wouldn't wake up to take him. His father had raced home after Edward had called him, swearing that she had been perfectly fine when he had left that morning, but the truth was she'd been dead for several hours. That was over a year ago. Now Edward found himself gasping, as he did most mornings when remembering that day.

Edward returned the framed photograph to the counter, wiping his eyes, and he picked up the second, a black-and-white one that Edward had taken with his Kodak Instamatic and developed himself in his late grandfather's darkroom. She was sitting in an inner tube on the Apple River, as gorgeous as a morning glory in her one-piece suit. She smiled proudly at the photographer, her son. The Apple River, in Wisconsin, meandered through farm country, past red barns and silos and tall fields of corn that Norman Rockwell could have painted, and if you rented inner tubes where the road met the river above Somerset, a ferry service would bring you back hours later, after you had whisked through the heart-pounding white-water section at the end. Edward and his parents spent the day floating down the river, limbs and buttocks in the cold, brownish water, sun warming skin like ruddy pears, and they chatted, laughed, splashed each other. At one point his mother stared at him and smiled brightly, kind of oddly, as if something were on her mind.

"What?" Edward said.

"I'm just soaking you in, like a sunflower does the sun."

"Why?"

"Come closer and I'll tell you." As he approached, she pulled his inner tube close to hers, brushed his hair with her fingers, then leaned over and whispered to him, "You're going to have a brother or sister!"

But that didn't come to be because of her fall. Nothing seemed to come to the way it was supposed to be. It seemed to him most movies got it wrong. Nothing is happily ever after.

Edward placed that photograph next to the other by the sink, and he now felt determined to at least make one small thing right. The very next knot seemed to do the job, with the large side flipped around the thin side twice, and then the fat side snaking up and then under. It looked like a knot. It slipped like a knot. That's all that mattered.

And for a few seconds, Edward felt as happy as an eagle swooping onto its prey. He had done it. He had figured it out. But he soon was angry again thinking how his father would march him off soon to McCory for another week. With classes until three, and sports until five, Edward did not get home until after six each night. A silent meal together, and then Edward would have two or three hours of homework before bed. Edward felt so alone, he wished he could be paint and just disappear onto the wall.

That morning at school, high on the hill, in the hallway that led to the chapel, Edward felt himself shoved forward, and as he whipped around, fat John De Bernieres laughed at him.

"You look a little sleepy this morning, stumbling around," De Bernieres said. He reached for Edward's tie and yanked, pulling Edward's neck in a jerk. The tie didn't come off, and Edward smiled, triumphant. "Oh, a *real* tie?" said De Bernieres. "You're keeping me on my toes, are you? Did Encyclopedia Man tie one for you?"

No one would have found out about his father's job if, last week, his father hadn't been in the school library delivering a new set, which he had sold to the school at cost. This only added to Edward's nightmare at the school. Now people knew his dad wasn't "in publishing" but was a salesman. Why did everything have to be so terrible? Why couldn't he just get by without people seeing him?

"What's a matter, Britannica?" said De Bernieres, egging him on. "Going to cry?"

Edward, his hand in a fist, leapt at the fat boy. Edward was going to show this slob to stay away, but De Bernieres was fast and stepped aside. Edward missed, and as he swung back around, De Bernieres stuck his fat foot out, and Edward fell forward, landing on his hands.

At that moment, the headmaster exited his office nearby. He saw Edward on the floor. "Come now," he said. "No fooling around, young man. Time for chapel." And the headmaster strode off.

"Yeah, Britannica. Time for chapel." And John De Bernieres waddled away. Edward stood as the bell for chapel rang. The stinging of his hands disappeared quickly, but one wrist throbbed and hurt. Soon the hallway was full of boys racing, like cattle down a chute from a railway car. Everyone was in a hurry, and Edward did not matter. Edward followed the young, suited group into the dark mahogany of the chapel, dimly lit by the flame-shaped bulbs on the chandeliers above. The chapel had an obsidian quality, a sense of darkness that carried Edward into his pew.

That night his father noticed him eating with his left hand. "Manners, Edward. Use your right hand."

Edward did, gingerly, but it was clear something hurt.

"What happened to your hand?" his father asked.

"I fell."

"How?"

"Maybe my foot hit some gum or something."

"Christ, can't you be more careful?" his father mumbled, stood up, and left as if to get something. He returned with an Ace bandage. "You know how this works, right?" said his father.

"Sure. I'll do it later." And Edward continued eating with his right hand, even though it felt like rats were eating at his tendons.

Later, when Edward went to get a glass of milk, his father was plotting a stock graph at the kitchen table, using closing prices from that day's newspaper. "How much homework do you have?" his father asked.

"I've been doing it."

"But how much do you have?"

"A lot."

"Okay, then. By the way, your Aunt Barbara is coming this weekend. She'll help out for a few weeks and have your bed, so you'll have to sleep in your sleeping bag again, okay?"

"All right." What was Edward going to do, demand Dad buy a guest bed at last? His father's sister, who once taught fifth grade in Duluth, Minnesota, had dark hair, sharp bangs, and an air of neglected beauty, like an original Ford Mustang, sun-baked, seats cracking. She felt compelled to visit a few times a year "to help out your father and make sure you get some mothering." Her idea of mothering was to shop at a school supply store and select maps of India or Crete for them to color. That was the most they did together; otherwise, she and his father went to restaurants, which Edward knew to be cocktail lounges, leaving Edward alone. They always came back stumbling while trying to be stoic.

That night Edward's hand throbbed, and at one point, after he woke up in the middle of the night, he couldn't feel his hand at all. He bolted upright, thinking he had just killed his hand somehow, and he groaned deeply. As he moved, his foot slammed against the wall, making a deep thumping sound. Clearly the Ace bandage had become a tourniquet, cutting off the blood to his appendage. He couldn't feel his fingers! Surely his hand was dead. He'd have to be rushed to the hospital and have it amputated, and then he'd have a fake metal one like a bad spy in *Mad* magazine. Not only would the boys at school still try to yank off his ties, but they'd kick off his fake hand and play keep away with it.

He flicked on the light, which made him see checkerboards. He felt hot, woozy. Oh, great. He probably had gangrene, too, and maybe more would be chopped off than just a hand. Was God toying with him like a mouse? No, God was the mouse. That left him to be what? Cheese. He hated being cheese.

Edward managed to unravel his Ace bandage, and the minute he did so, his fingers started tingling, but he thought what's a hand going to do for him in this world? He now wanted to vomit, but if he did so, his father would probably make him not only wash the floor, but also all the bed linen, and he'd be up all night. Life was unfair.

As Edward lay in his bed, the one Aunt Barbara would soon get, he could hear footsteps. It was his father. Christ, he'd woken up his father somehow, and now he would get his wrath. Big shit. Edward had nothing more to hope for anyway.

"What the hell's going on with all the noise back here?" his father said at the doorway, eyes blinking from the light.

"Yeah, what the hell?" said Edward, not really thinking about what he verbalized.

"Are you all right?"

"Nothing that a new metal hand won't fix."

"What? Let me see." He sat on Edward's bed, causing Edward to slide toward him. One of Edward's legs rested against one of his father's legs. Edward felt his father lift his arm and feel his wrist. "Nothing feels broken. You just tied it too tight. I'd asked you if you knew how to use it."

"Oh, cut it off, what do I care?"

"What's gotten into you?"

"I'm a McCory boy, Dad. We rule the world!"

"Have you been drinking?"

"Like you when your sister's here?"

"What's wrong with you?" His father looked so instantly upset, Edward thought he might slap him, but instead his father leaned in and smelled his breath. His father frowned, and then looked concerned. Edward felt the cool of his father's palm on his forehead.

"You're burning up" his father said, surprise cutting into his usual exasperation. "You just need some aspirin. That's all you need. I'll get you some aspirin, okay?"

"Is that all I need, Dad?"

"What are you talking about?"

"I hate McCory."

"You have to give it a chance."

"Whatever you say, *Sir!*"

"You have a high fever, and aspirin will cut it. High fevers make you say strange things."

"Just leave me alone like you did Mom. I'll die quietly in the night."

His father raised a hand as if to strike. In seeing his own hand raised, he turned away as if aghast, clutching his own, terrible hand. He then whispered, "What do you want from me? I try to do the best, don't you understand?"

"Mom died because of you, right?" spat Edward, wanting his father to hit him.

His father sat on the bed, bent over like a question mark, looking away still, nodding his head, and his whole body joined in. Was he crying?

"Sometimes I think yes. Yeah," whispered his father, covering his eyes.

Edward stared, numb, as if just witnessing the Wayzata train derailing into the bay.

"Your mother—she was special, and I'm sorry I can't be her," continued his father. "I'm so sorry things haven't worked out as either one of us expected. I miss her so terribly much."

"Me, too."

"I know. I wish I could be like her, but I'm not. And even if I were like her, would that make up for her leaving us?"

Edward felt tears in his eyes, but he didn't care. He let them fall. He saw, too, his father's face now, and his eyes were watery. Edward wasn't sure who leaned in first—maybe both together at the same time—but they hugged.

"Maybe you don't understand this, Edward, but I easily love you as much as anyone on this earth, including your mother."

"You do?"

"I do."

Edward felt stunned, as if he were a pupil of Aristotle's, learning that the world was not flat but round. "I love you, too, Dad."

They each wiped their eyes quickly—they were men, after all—and his father left the room. Edward could hear him rummaging in the kitchen, where the aspirin was kept, and a few minutes later he returned with two tablets and a glass of water. Edward swallowed the pills, drank extra water, and placed the glass on his nightstand. His father tucked him in. "Everything will be all right. Trust me."

"Will it?" said Edward. Through the window, a crescent of the moon appeared just above the trees.

His father leaned over and kissed Edward on his forehead— the first kiss since his mother had died.

Acknowledgements:

I balance my writing life with teaching, and I'm fueled by the talent I see. Thank you to the chairs, deans, directors and students in my life that lend gravity to my orbit. In particular, my appreciation goes to deans Susan Kamei and Jane Cody as well as Ebony Cunningham and Natalie Kaylor at USC's Master of Professional Writing program; to CalArts character animation program director Cynthia Overman and to Martha Baxton, Jennifer Jeremich, and the staff in the film school office; to film school dean Steve Anker and president Steven Lavine at CalArts for a completion grant to help publish this book—their support means much; to dean Mark Breitenberg, director Julia Hurr, and the staff at the Art Center College of Design; to English program chair Susan Sterr and the staff at Santa Monica College; to Linda Venis and the staff at UCLA Extension. I don't teach at all of these places at any given time, but this reflects the modern professor, flying on the freeways. My destinations are good ones.

Many writers are not lonely. I'm not. Thank you to my many friends and my wife, Ann, and to Roderick Clark of *Rosebud* magazine, who has supported my short fiction over the years by publishing my stories. Thank you to Carol Fass and her wonderful publicity agency and to Carol Fuchs for her proofreading. A toast to my agent, Jim McCarthy, for his wise counsel. A thousand thanks to book designer Daniel Will-Harris and book editor Nomi Kleinmuntz.

Printed in the United States
217046BV00001B/64/P